# Ocean's Justice

DEMELZA CARLTON

# DEDICATION

*This book is dedicated to Oma, for inspiring me to immortalise toilet paper. No shipboard birthday is complete without it.*

# One

If I never saw the sea again, it would be too soon.

"She's too much trouble. Too turbulent to do what she must. Send her away somewhere so she can learn obedience. Then she may return."

"She's too young — barely eighteen. She's still upset over his death. Surely we should wait before we send her anywhere."

"No. She did what needed to be done and he's dead by her hand. She's understandably upset, but that will fade. He was only a man. I say we send her away and see what she's capable of accomplishing. What say you, child?"

My mouth still tasted bad at the words I'd spat at the vicious old women, but I'd say the same thing again in a heartbeat. "I hate you. I loved him. He didn't deserve to die and I will NEVER obey your orders again."

My defiance was futile. What did it get me? A small raft drifting across the Indian Ocean, with nothing but the sound of waves and the smell of salt and coal-smoke.

Smoke meant a ship. I was saved.

I squinted into the sunlight, but the waves hid the vessel from me. Maybe I was looking the wrong way. I didn't have the strength to sit up and see.

Rough hands seized me. I struggled, but my weakness won.

Blue eyes drifted above, the same colour as the ocean below. A tangle of wiry seaweed obscured the rest of the man's face.

"It's all right, lass. I'll take care of you."

Darkness took me first.

# Two

"Miss? Can you tell me your name? Can you even hear me?" A clammy hand touched my forehead.

I focussed on the words and tried to translate them. I responded to the only one I understood. "Maria."

"Your name is Maria?"

My neck felt stiff as I nodded and opened my eyes.

"I'm Charlie. Charles Seaborn, but everyone calls me Charlie. The other men said you wouldn't live, but Mr McGregor said any girl who could rig that raft and survive long enough to be rescued wasn't going to die in her bed. Mr Allchin, the cook, is going to be furious when he finds out I won my bet. When we reach the Cape, I'm going to use the money to pay for my first woman and…beg pardon, miss. Maria, I mean." The boy reddened, but it didn't slow his words. "Some of the other men are saying you're something supernatural, seeing as you look like Venus and all, on account of having no clothes. Not like them skinny flappers. You have bosoms. The men talk about them a lot. A few say you're bad luck and we never should have rescued you, because you'll doom us like your last ship, but if you were going to sink ships, you wouldn't be floating around on a raft with no clothes and no food or water, a breath away from death. Doesn't make sense. Are you hungry, miss?"

Charlie held out a round, flat piece of metal, topped with a smaller, brown, oval slab. "It's bread, miss. Bread with marmite." He broke a small piece off the slab and popped it into his mouth. He pulled a face. "I don't like marmite – my mum makes me eat it for my health, she says, and Mr Allchin says you must eat it so you don't get beri-beri after so long at sea. Can you remember the name of your ship?"

I still didn't understand his words – but I did register that the slab was food. I reached for it, inclining my head in gratitude to the boy, before I gingerly took my first bite of marmite sandwich. It was the consistency of sponge and it tasted like the sea, but I chewed, swallowed and forced myself to take another bite. My mouth was as dry as dune sand and the additional salt didn't help. Swallowing was painful.

"Drink, miss?" Charlie held out a cup of liquid.

I seized it and sat up, tipping the cup's contents into my mouth. The second mouthful of salty, sponge-like sandwich went down far more smoothly than the first. I wished for the sweet flesh of a fresh fish, but it looked like only marmite was on the menu, whatever that might be.

A choking noise made me look up at Charlie's red face. He seemed to be staring at my chest. "Um, miss? Maria? The Captain found some clothes for you, seeing as you don't have any. Men's clothes, as we're all men here. To protect your…modesty, miss." The boy reddened further as his hands described the curves he couldn't tear his eyes away from.

The rough blanket that had previously covered my body now bared my skin to the waist, so I pulled it up again. This seemed to break the boy from his trance and he stepped away to retrieve a small pile of folded fabric. He shook out a creamy-coloured item that turned out to be a shirt similar to his, which he held out to me. I took the shirt and slipped it over my head, thankful that I didn't have to fumble with the shell buttons under his watchful eyes, for they were already fastened. Next came the pants, which were almost identical to those he wore — including the length of rope threaded through the belt loops. I shifted to the edge of the bunk, so I could put these on, too. The sight of my bare legs seemed to mesmerise the boy almost as much as my breasts had. Perhaps he'd never seen either before.

The pants were much too wide at the waist — I had to hold them up to prevent them from puddling around my ankles. I pulled on the rope, ending up with the length of hemp in my hand and the waist of my pants clutched in the other.

"Ooh, miss, you have to thread it back through those bits there and then tighten it with both ends and cross the ends over and…" Charlie's hands gestured as he attempted to illustrate the words I didn't understand. Bewildered, I tried to follow his hand movements, but the pants slid down and hit the deck.

Deep laughter erupted from behind Charlie and we both turned to see who found my ineptitude funny. What I'd mistaken for seaweed was the man's bristly beard, now tamed to a short pelt across his chin and upper lip. Ocean-blue eyes regarded me with amusement as the man who owned them strode into the cabin. "Caught with your pants down, boy. Very compromising for the lady's honour, especially when we don't even know her name."

"Oh, no, Mr McGregor, you see, she was putting her clothes on and I was trying to help, only I don't think she's worn men's clothes before and these don't fit so well and I couldn't explain how to tie a rope belt and…" The boy continued with his endless sentence-story without pausing for breath, but Blue Eyes had eyes for no one but me.

His gaze was frankly curious, but arrogant, too, in a way that turned my confusion and fear to courage. I straightened, returning his gaze with all the pride of my position. No matter what I wore or where I stood, I wouldn't let this man cow me. Instead, I wanted to tell him to stop his insolent scrutiny. As I lacked the words in his language, I let my stare convey the message for me.

Charlie fell silent and moved aside. Blue Eyes stood before me, close enough to touch, yet he didn't lift his hand nor break the lock that held his eyes and mine. "I think this lady has a lot more honour at stake than we first thought. My lady, what's your name?"

I opened my mouth to answer, but I found my throat too dry to make a sound. This man did strange things to my body with merely his voice and his eyes.

"Maria," Charlie supplied. "That's the only thing she's said. But she was so hungry she ate a whole marmite sandwich and drank all the water."

"Fetch some more water for Lady Maria, boy. And tell Captain Foster she's awake and receiving visitors."

Charlie nodded rapidly. "Yes, Mr McGregor." He hurried out.

Blue Eyes dropped to a crouch at my feet, gathering up my pants. "Permit me to assist you, Lady Maria. We have no maids and no other women aboard, but I'll do the best I can." He pulled the fabric up to my waist, snaking the rope through the loops and tightening it in one swift move, taking my breath away. "On second thought, you should probably tuck this shirt in. That way, it will hide your assets better." His hand stroked my shirt against my skin, smoothing it beneath the waistband of my pants. Heat flooded my body at every caress and my heart beat faster still.

NO! This man wasn't Giuseppe and I wouldn't betray his memory with this strange man, despite his warm hands and ocean-coloured eyes.

He noticed my sudden stiffness and said, "I'm sorry, Lady Maria, but I'm not used to dressing ladies. You must think me very clumsy. I don't mean to take liberties. I'll be as quick as I can." He tied the rope at my waist, avoiding touching me again. "There."

The pants hung from my hips, but they didn't fall, and the shirt ballooned out from my shoulders to my waist, almost hiding my breasts completely. I looked like him and Charlie now. I wanted to thank him, but I didn't know the words to use. Nor did I know Blue Eyes' name.

I patted my chest, as Charlie had when he told me his name. "Name Maria," I said, wishing I knew more of his language.

"I'm delighted to meet you, Lady Maria, and I hope you don't think too badly of us for offering the best we have. If we knew we'd have a female passenger aboard, we might've…"

I shook my head, tears of frustration springing to my eyes. "No lady. Name Maria. Name?" In desperation, I reached out and touched the front of his shirt. I felt hard muscle beneath. "Name?"

He glanced down at my hand before meeting my eyes. "You mean I've seen you undressed, touched your body and helped you dress, but I haven't had the good manners to tell you my name? Good God, what you must think of me. I'm so sorry." He covered my hand with his. "My name's William McGregor, lass, and I'm not normally such a brute. I don't know if you remember, but 'twas I who pulled you off that raft. We thought you were dead, but I swore I'd check anyway, and I was never so relieved to see those blue eyes of yours staring up at me in terror. I didn't mean to frighten you then, lass — but you gave us all a good scare first."

So many words that I wished I knew the meaning of. I tried to repeat the ones I wanted. "Will…William. Mug….Mug…" I closed my eyes in defeat. I hadn't understood the man's name — I'd lost it.

I felt his fingers tighten around mine. "That's right, lass. You can just call me William if you like. Much easier than McGregor for those who aren't used to it. Unless you tell me your family's name, I'll be calling you by your

Christian name, too, so it's fitting."

I bowed my head, feeling my lips lift in a smile for the first time since Giuseppe died. "William."

# Three

"She's awake and up and about, just like Charlie said. I thought the boy was exaggerating, yet here she is. Good to see you survived your ordeal, miss," the older man with a peaked cap said as he stepped into the tiny cabin. He held his hand out to me. "Captain Foster of the *Trevessa*, miss."

I took his hand, as I knew was the custom, and swallowed. "Maria, Captain Foster."

"Can you tell us what happened, Maria? How did you come to be floating on that raft in the middle of the ocean? There are no ships reported missing, though with the storms we've seen since we left Fremantle, it's surprising. Were you on a smaller vessel – a yacht, perhaps?" Captain Foster asked.

I looked from one man to the other, wishing I could answer, but I didn't understand a word. Both men seemed to be waiting for me to say something, yet I had no idea what.

Captain Foster coughed. "Half the crew are saying that you're some kind of sea monster, that you murdered everyone aboard your last ship before you sank it and that you'll do the same here. Are you here to kill us all, Maria?"

"Captain!" William roared so loudly that I jumped. "The girl's been through quite an ordeal. I hardly think you should be accusing her of things only a superstitious native would believe."

The captain's voice remained calm. "Yet you're the one shocked, not her. Either she did sink her last ship or the girl doesn't understand a word I just said. You don't speak English, do you, Maria?" His eyes appeared to bore into mine, as if he might extract his answers this way. I stared back calmly. I needed to learn their language so that I could communicate – if only to tell this man that I didn't understand. He cleared his throat. "German, maybe. *Fräulein, Sie sind hier, um uns zu töten?* Or Dutch - *mevrouw, bent u hier om ons te doden?*" (Miss, are you here to kill us?)

I understood a little of this and tried to reply. "*Niet doden. Levend.*" (Not dead. Alive.)

Captain Foster burst out laughing. "By God, her Dutch is worse than mine. We pick up a shipwrecked girl and she can't understand a word we say, nor tell us what happened. What do you suggest, McGregor? You fished her up."

"I'll go up against any man who wants to throw her back," William said fiercely.

The captain seemed uncomfortable as he shifted position. "It may come to that. They're a suspicious lot and the fog when we left Fremantle made many of us uneasy. I have a ship to run and no time to protect the girl. This ship is no place for a woman, but while we have one on board…"

"I'll take care of her, captain. After all, I'm just a passenger aboard your ship – what else do I have to do during the voyage? At least she's easy on the eyes and she doesn't say much." William extended his elbow toward me and I stared at it, uncertain of what he wanted. After a moment, he took my hand and laid it on his forearm. "I'll show her the mess, so she knows where to find what passes for food on this tub." Towing me behind him, he led the way along a metal tunnel and up the ladder to where I could hear the clamour of many voices. William smiled at me, tightening his grip on my hand. "Time to introduce you to the rest of the crew, lass. Just flash that pretty smile and you'll enchant them all, same as you have me."

I swallowed and passed through the doorway with him. A few heads turned to stare and silence fell.

"This is Maria, lads. Now, she doesn't say much and we don't think she speaks English, but that's no excuse not to treat her like the lady she is." Benches scraped across the deck as every man in the room rose — more than thirty of them, I guessed. I smiled and inclined my head in response to what I recognised as a gesture of respect. "That's right. She's been through a lot before we found her on that bit of flotsam she used for a raft, so remember your manners and help the lady if she needs it."

One man said something in a low voice, his hands describing enormous breasts in front of his own flat chest. The man beside him guffawed loudly, which drew the attention of many other men.

"Anyone who doesn't show her proper respect will answer to me," William continued, fixing his gaze on the two men who'd made noise.

Silence lasted for a few seconds more before William pulled me toward the back of the room. The scents of what the men were eating intensified with each step toward the source — a counter that held metal pans of unfamiliar food. No, not all. One held…"Beras!" I exclaimed, recognising the rice.

The white-hatted man behind the counter stared at me. "If she eats that, she'll get beri-beri. She needs to eat more of my marmite…" He reached down and produced a large jar filled with the unpleasant paste I'd eaten earlier.

I stared the man in the eye and shook my head. I pointed at the rice.

William laughed and passed me a metal plate. "Allchin, if the lady wants rice, that's what she gets. She might want a taste of your stew, too. I'll take my serving of stew with bread, thank you."

Allchin ladled a thick, lumpy, brown liquid onto William's plate and handed him two slices of bread. I received a mound of rice, which was quickly swamped by a sea of brown liquid. "Looks like the demon's tit, where you're going, McGregor," Allchin said, nodding at my plate. "Christmas Island, paradise for bird crap and crabs."

William laughed again. "I've heard those crabs are good eating. It'll be a damn sight better than your cooking, man." He grabbed some clinking metal things and guided me to the empty end of one table.

With a quick glance at the other men, I climbed onto the bench seat as William sat across from me. His handful of metal implements clattered to the table in front of me and I reached for them, directing a questioning look at William. He nodded and seized one with pointed tines at one end. He stabbed a brown lump on his plate and lifted it to his mouth.

That was fine for him with his plate full of large chunks of food but spearing the rice seemed like an exercise in futility. I looked down the table and was relieved to see a dark-haired man using a tool with a shallow depression on its end to shovel rice and liquid into his mouth. I picked up a spoon and cautiously scraped a little of the food onto it. My hand shook as I lifted it to my mouth.

The texture was mushy and the taste was bland, to say the least. I chewed and swallowed, spooning a slightly larger serving for my next mouthful. This was nothing like the food from home, which I might never taste again. Warm tears spilled down my cheeks and I wiped them away, not wanting to show weakness in front of so many strangers.

"Not as good as home cooking, is it, lass?" William asked, grinning over a large mouthful of food. His eyes held sympathy, as if he could read my thoughts.

I managed to smile, before laboriously continuing with my meal.

"I should get you some tea," William said, rising. I moved to follow him, but he gestured for me to sit down.

He returned with two cups of steaming, red-brown liquid. "Just the way I like it — brewed thick, like it is in the mining office back home.

The tea lady used to say that the bottom of the teapot was still tarred by the first leaves when the mine opened, a century ago."

I accepted the cup and lifted it to my lips.

"No, wait! You'll burn yourself if you —" He tried to snatch the cup from my fingers.

Too late. My mouthful of hot liquid burned both my tongue and the roof of my mouth, but I couldn't emit my wail of pain without spitting the tea in William's face. Whimpering, I swallowed, feeling the heat slide down my throat. Betrayed, I stared at William. Had he intended to hurt me?

His stricken expression told me the answer, followed by his anguished tone as he said, "Did you hurt yourself? I'm so sorry. I didn't realise you wouldn't know what to do with tea. Here, you sip it slowly, like this." He lifted his own cup and slurped a small amount of liquid. I scanned his face for signs of distress or pain, but there was none. "You try it." He took another tiny sip.

I cautiously grasped my cup again and

brought it to my mouth with both shaking hands. Slowly, I tipped it so that a tiny trickle hit my tongue. Now it didn't burn me – but I could taste the foul brew. It was like drinking diluted mangrove mud. I think I preferred the burn to the taste. Yet, in the face of William's desperate expression, I drank it anyway and was rewarded by his nervous smile.

"My mum always said a cup of tea could soothe all the troubles in the world. No matter how far from home we are, at least there's tea," he said.

"Tea?" I enquired, pointing at our cups.

William grinned. "An important word to remember, lass. Where there's tea, there's civilisation."

Trying not to grimace, I drank the stuff, wondering what kind of backward people willingly drank river mud.

# Four

Once dinner was over, William escorted me back to my cabin. I noticed he braced his arms against the bulkheads as he walked, to maintain his balance as the ship moved in the stormy swell, and I found myself doing the same. The ship's motion made my stomach queasy, but the feeling soon passed as I learned to move with the ship. After all, my tiny raft had moved far more in the waves and I'd managed to sleep on that. I hummed quietly to myself as we walked, feeling my body relax further as the soothing song did its work.

When we reached my cabin, William closed the door and turned to face me. His face seemed paler than before. He covered his mouth quickly, as if he were attempting to mask the sound of his belch. "Beg pardon, lass." He swallowed a couple of times before he continued, "The captain and I agreed that it'd be best if I stayed here tonight. For your safety, of course."

Between his troubled expression, darkened eyes and rigid stance, I found grounds for a strong premonition of danger. Something was wrong and I didn't trust this stranger enough. I pointed at him, then extended my arm toward the door. "Go," I said.

He stood firm, shaking his head. "No go. Whether you like it or not, lass, you won't budge me. You'll be sleeping in the upper bunk tonight and I'll take the one below you." His pointed finger stabbed at me, the upper bunk, himself and the lower bunk, while his angry eyes challenged me.

I held his gaze for a few long seconds, before deciding to scramble up the ladder to the top bunk. I stretched out on the thin mattress, suddenly realising how tired I was. The ship moved in the waves, rocking me like a mother would a fretful baby. I opened my eyes to find William watching me.

"Rest, Maria. I swear you have nothing to fear from me. I'll be a right gentleman, here below you." With slow, deliberate movements, he lay down on the lower bunk, where I'd been sleeping only a few hours before. "I know you don't know a thing about me, but I'd change that if I could. How about I tell you a little about myself? Let me know if you grow bored, lass." His voice became gentler and more reflective.

Deciding I must have imagined the risk, I relaxed. I was hardly helpless — as he'd find out if he did pose a danger to me. In the meantime, I'd conserve my energy and listen to his melodic voice.

"I have two brothers and a sister. While all

three of them were content to stay in Scotland, working, marrying and bringing up their children as McGregors have been doing for centuries, I was never content. I wanted adventure, like I read in my books. Too young to enlist in the Great War, I did my engineering studies with many other lads who were eager to work on all the new technological advances. Warships, weapons, vehicles that could travel further and faster than anything we'd ever seen. My best friend was a lad who'd lived in Japan for all his life – Japanese mother, English father. He was fascinated by improving land for higher crop yields – he said with all the new scientific discoveries in chemistry, we could grow enough food for everyone and no one would ever starve again. Crazy, I tell you – but it turned out his father was a partner in a shipping venture which shipped some of these miracle growth agents to Japan. The chemicals come from mines and extracting the raw material is quite an undertaking. So when he heard of a position on the other side of the world, he thought of me. He and his father wrote letters to some very important people and the next thing I knew, I was hired to run a guano mine in a place I've never heard of. But first, I had to be trained to represent Britain in its colonies, for that's what this place is. All it did was scare the hell out of me.

"A few weeks at the Imperial Institute in London, on the Tropical African Administrative Service training course and I'm supposed to be an expert at managing a new colony. I'm an engineer. I know steam and mining, like my father and my grandfather. There are so many insects that can kill you in Africa, I don't know half the names. And no one's ever heard of the place I'm going — except to tell horrible stories about it. They say there are crabs there — bigger than coconuts — that can crack your head open as you sleep…" The words faded as the man retched and I heard liquid spatter. He coughed and said, "Beg pardon, lass. No one told me I'd be sick as a dog on the sea. Give me land and I'll never leave it again. I imagine you feel the same way."

I peered over the side of the bunk, just in time to see him set the bucket on the floor and wipe his mouth with the back of his hand.

"One good thing about tasteless food is that it's not so bad bringing it back up again. I learned that in the North Atlantic, fresh out of Liverpool. Captain Foster said that the storm was something called a hurricane. The Americans can keep the damned things, I tell you, lass…"

His deep, purring voice continued, lulling me to sleep. I came to understand that "lass" was his name for me and I wondered what it meant. I slipped into a doze, feeling comfortable for the first time.

A creak and a clunk jerked me from sleep to alertness. The door swung open against the bulkhead and a shadow blocked the corridor lights.

"Women aboard ship is bad luck," a new voice growled. The sound was menacing and my eyes scanned the room in search of a weapon. The hulking new man grumbled some more, but his words meant as much to me as the rumbling steam engine beneath us. More worrying were the steps he took into the room – approaching the bunks.

I drew in a silent breath, steeling myself for whatever I'd need to do in order to defend myself.

The man leaned over the lower bunk and seized William. "Send you back to the ocean where you belong," the man grunted, trying to lift him.

In a flurry of blankets, William delivered a blow to the man – whether from his fist or foot, I couldn't tell – and sent him crashing against the bulkhead. William's fist caught the man under the chin next, jerking his head up before his whole body slid down the wall to slump on the deck.

"Get out of here, Barrett. If I ever see you near the girl again, I'll break your jaw and throw you overboard instead."

The man – Barrett, I presumed – scrambled to his feet and staggered to the doorway, holding onto the bulkhead as he struggled to remain upright. "The girl will curse and kill us all, McGregor. She's a siren, sent to seduce us and sink the ship. You're defending a monster."

"Shut your mouth before I break some more of your teeth. Maria's been through enough. She doesn't need to hear your superstitious nonsense and nor do I. Go make yourself useful and stoke the boiler. The sooner we get to shore the sooner you'll be shot of her – and me, too. Until then – if you have anything to say to her, you can say it to me and I'll decide if she needs to hear it or if I need to smash your face." I didn't understand William's angry words, but his meaning was clear – he pointed at the door and the other man left, spitting bitterly on the deck.

Strange – both here tonight and on the mess deck, I'd seen the other men regard William with an odd mixture of contempt and respect. Much like I regarded my elders, the women who had sent me so far from home. Yet this man didn't seem much older than I. I wished I could ask him how he'd earned a reputation that made the larger man back down, or the whole crew stand up, as they had in the mess.

I was surprised to feel William's warm hand over mine.

"Like I said, I'll make sure no harm comes to you, lass. I may be ill, but I'm still a match for any man on this crew."

I stared at William until I became lost in his liquid eyes and he laughed at me. His laughter lit a warmth inside me that I hadn't felt since Giuseppe – but Giuseppe was dead by my hands. He would never touch me again and I vowed no other man would, either. My heart and my love belonged to a dead man.

"Good night, Maria."

I didn't dare speak a word – I understood so little of what he said and needed to learn so much before I could communicate.

# Five

What if I could never return home again? What if I had to make my life with these people, in a world I didn't understand? Alone. I hugged my knees to my chest, peering out the porthole at the matching grey sky and seas. I could do what Barrett had suggested last night – throw myself into the waves and let the ocean take me.

William knocked on the bulkhead beside me, startling me out of my gloomy thoughts. "I brought you a gift, lass. Something no lady should be without." He held out a piece of tortoiseshell, carved into a row of teeth. "I bought this for my sister. I meant to send it to her before we left Fremantle, but I forgot. Now it's yours."

I took the gift from him, smiling my thanks.

"I don't mean to sound rude, but I think the words you're after are, 'Thank you.'" He imitated my smile and the way I bowed my head, then raised his voice to a high-pitched squeak. "Thank you, William."

I stared at him, then slowly repeated the words. "Th…thank you, William."

"You're welcome, lass. Now, I have a favour to ask. An ulterior motive, perhaps." He paused, but I didn't say a word, so he continued, "Back home, they say a girl with her hair unbound is unleashing a storm to sink ships at sea. Maybe that's just the North Sea and the Indian Ocean's too big to be controlled by a woman's hair, but it makes me nervous and Captain Foster's been worried since we left port. Would you…would you please pin your hair up?" He coughed. "If you don't know how, would you let me do it? The sister I bought the comb for…I used to help her with her hair before school in the mornings. She said I had gentler hands than Mum." He sat beside me on the bed and lifted a cautious hand toward my hair. He stroked the salt-encrusted length of it, right down to the ends lying on the bed beside me. "Now, I heard one of the Singhs asking Allchin for some cooking oil for his hair, so while Allchin was serving breakfast, I liberated some for you." He lifted a large can that I hadn't noticed until now and he shook it, so I could hear the slosh of a little liquid inside. "Would you…would you like me to help you?"

I looked at him, longing to be able to answer him – or even understand his question.

"I wish you could understand me. I'm sure you'll let me know if you want me to stop." He lifted the can over my head and I felt something trickle through my hair. I kept my eyes on William's scared smile, hoping I didn't look equally nervous. He set the can down with a clatter and lifted both hands to my head. "I suppose I just have to spread this through your hair." He threaded his fingers through my hair, gently massaging my scalp with his fingertips, then smoothed my hair between his hands.

I closed my eyes, enjoying the sensation. No one had ever touched me like this. Not my mother, not my friends, not even Giuseppe. A quiet moan of pleasure escaped from my lips and my eyes shot open, staring at William in panic.

He chuckled. "I believe that's a most emphatic 'yes'. More, Maria?"

A word I understood! I beamed. "Yes. Oh, yes, William. Thank you."

He leaned closer to me. "You should turn around, so I can reach your hair better. If you moan like that again, God help me, but I'm going to have to kiss you." He wrapped his hands around my hair, pulling it toward him, and I twisted my body away from his to make it easier. "That's probably safest. Comb?"

I felt William pluck the comb from my fingers and start stroking it through my hair, pulling the tangles from my tresses. He said, "My sister used to tell me all her troubles when I did her hair. As if the comb loosened her tongue. I doubt you'll be as forthcoming, but if you have anything you wish to say, I'm listening, lass."

Wishing I had some way of thanking him for his kindness, I stared down at my body, covered in borrowed clothes. This was all I had and something in the hesitant way he touched me told me that my body wasn't the sort of currency he'd accept. But what else did I have to offer?

The ship rolled beneath us and I clutched at the bunk to avoid being pitched onto the floor, remembering William's illness last night. There was one thing I could offer.

My voice quiet and quivering at first, I lifted it in the same soothing song I'd hummed last night – the one that had calmed my unsettled stomach. Breathing deeper, I increased the volume, putting more power into my voice. This song reminded me of home and the family I might never see again, but it was also the sound of comfort, for my mother had sung the same melody for as long as I could remember. Once I'd started, I couldn't stop. I sang of loss and grief, but I also sang of hope, for the unexpected bliss this man held in his skilful hands.

I let the last note hang in the air before I silenced it, wishing there was more I could offer him.

William lifted my hair, laying it over my shoulder, and placed the end in my hand. I looked down and saw the satin ribbon that bound the braided length – braided just like the rope that Giuseppe had tried and failed to hold on to in the surging waves. The waves that had stolen him from me and drowned him. I burst into tears.

"Here – here." William's arms folded around me, almost crushing me to his chest. I'd never been held so securely – never felt this safe with anyone. "I didn't think I did such a bad job. You look beautiful, Maria, and with your amazing voice and lovely song, you've absolutely bewitched me. The crew will stop calling you a sea monster now they see how beautiful you are. They'll call you an enchantress instead."

Embarrassed, I tried to stem the flood. I swallowed hard, staring fixedly at the fishbone pattern of my braid. He had done me another kindness and I'd responded by soaking his shirt with silly tears. "Thank you, William," I said steadily. "Thank you."

William's grip on me tightened as he reached into his pocket and withdrew a folded piece of cloth. Pressing the handkerchief into my hand, he replied, "Any time, lass. The song alone was worth it. Now let's hope we've seen the end of storms for this voyage." He seemed thoughtful for a moment, before he added, "How'd you like me to give you a grand tour of the ship?"

I heard the question in his tone, but he could have been asking me for anything. Staring into his eyes, I found myself nodding.

He took my hand. "Then come with me."

# Six

As we headed down the corridor toward the washroom, he tucked my arm under his, laying my fingers across his cotton-clad forearm. "The washroom you know," he said, waving his hand at the empty room. "There's another on the other side of the ship, where most of the crew sleep, for only the captain's quarters have running water. Captain's quarters are two doors down from ours." He pointed at a closed door, then turned into a corridor I hadn't used before and rounded a corner.

"Here – crew quarters." William led me into a corridor almost identical to the one where our cabin was, only this had far more doors, much closer together.

I heard the sounds of splashing and raised men's voices, then laughter as a pale, gangly figure burst into the corridor.

"That's not funny! Those are the last pants I have, what with loaning one pair to Maria and all!" Charlie shouted reedily, the muscles in his bare backside clenching as he drew himself up. He turned, caught sight of us, and emitted a very feminine shriek as he tried to cover his genitals with his hands. One hand would have sufficed in the cold morning air.

I burst out laughing, which made Charlie's face turn red.

"Mr McGregor, you could have warned us," Charlie complained, edging back into the washroom. "Miss Maria shouldn't see men when we're…when we're…" His words were drowned out by a wave of loud laughter from inside the washroom.

I advanced, but William grabbed my arm. His cheeks were flushed, too. "Probably not the best place for a lady like yourself. We get pretty rowdy without women present and some of the men are in no fit state to be seen. We'd better start with the hold." His voice sounded uneasy and I wondered what I'd done to unsettle him. Was it my laughter at Charlie's unfortunate shrinkage? Surely he hadn't expected me to admire the modestly endowed boy.

William led the way silently down ladders and corridors until we were in the echoing bowels of the ship. Here, overhead lights provided all the illumination – no natural light percolated to this depth. He fastened his hands on a wheel set in the middle of a metal door and wrenched the wheel around. Several squeaky turns later, William pulled the wheel toward him and the door swung open with a protesting creak. "This is the cargo hold. Some sort of mineral Australia's shipping to Belgium for the factories there. It looks like the mud we pump out of the coal mines back home – not useful at all!" He pulled a tube out of his pocket and a weak beam of light shot out of the end of it, splashing against the far wall of the hold. Beneath the beam was a pool of dark mud, bounded by walls and a metal catwalk that ran around the edges of the large space. The light beam rose to illuminate the hatch in the ceiling. "One of the port inspectors fell through the hatch before they sealed it. He almost drowned before they pulled him out – that stuff is like quicksand. It'll suck you under without a trace if no one hears you scream."

The mud held little interest for me, but William's hand-held light tube was fascinating. I dropped to my knees, reaching for the metal length he held at waist height. He laughed and clicked the device, extinguishing the light before another click blinded me as the bulb glowed to life. "It's a torch, lass."

"Torch?" I ventured, laying my hand on the surprisingly warm metal.

William's hand covered mine, pressing my

finger down until a click turned the torch off. "If you want to play with it for a bit, it's all yours."

"Mr McGregor!" Charlie's voice leaped so high it broke. "What are you doing with Miss Maria?"

William stared down at me in shock for a moment before he jumped back, putting several feet between us. He waved the torch. "Showing her the hold and my torch, lad. Nothing…nothing inappropriate. She wanted a closer look at my torch and I didn't realise…if I'd thought how compromising it might look, I wouldn't have…" The front of his pants looked decidedly tight and uncomfortable.

Perhaps William wasn't as immune to my body as I'd thought, I reflected as I accepted Charlie's assistance to rise to my feet. I averted my eyes from the man's frantic, furtive wardrobe adjustments and followed Charlie instead.

The boy's hair was still wet, but he wore clothes as he led the way up the ladder. "You should see the engines, Miss Maria," he said eagerly. "The boiler room where the firemen work is like hell, but when you see how fast they stoke the engines – oh! It's like magic. You won't believe something so huge can go so fast."

William's muffled laugh behind me told me he was following us. "Lad, you have no idea," he muttered so quietly that I barely heard him, "but I think she might."

# Seven

I stepped over the threshold and into a raging inferno. The heat hit me first, searing the very breath in my lungs. Reflected flames danced along the walls and in the sheen of blackened sweat on the men who fed the real fire that heated the boilers.

My memory stirred, sparked and burst into horrifyingly clear images of the *Emden* burning as dying men screamed…and so did I.

"It's all right, lass." William's arms closed around me, pressing my body against his so that all I could see were the blurred folds of his shirt. "Charlie was only joking about it being hell, weren't you, lad? This is the boiler room, where the firemen stoke the fires to heat the boilers that drive the ship. Nothing to fear here. The lad – we both thought you'd like to see the powerful engines speeding us to land. If you don't want to, there's no harm done. Do you want to see more of the ship, Maria?"

I looked up and glimpsed the ruddy light before I squeezed my eyes shut. "No. No more," I replied, shaking my head.

William half-carried me out into the corridor and I felt the welcome relief of the cool bulkhead beside me. Sucking in a calming breath, I drew myself up and looked into the boiler room. The hard-working men inside eyed me curiously, between furiously shovelling coal into the well-contained fire. The flames weren't consuming any part of this ship, except for the plentiful coal that fed its roaring boilers. As for the *Emden*…she was nothing but a burned-out hulk by now.

"What's wrong, Miss Maria? Don't you want to see the engines?" Charlie blocked the boiler room doorway, looking crushed.

William saved me from having to answer. "All that talk of hell must have frightened her, lad. I don't think she's ever seen anything like it. Now I'm going to take her up to the main deck for some much-needed fresh air, I think." He nudged me toward the ladder to the deck above and I closed grateful fingers on the handrail as I climbed, feeling the vibration from William's weight not far below me.

"Wait for me!" called Charlie as I reached the upper deck, his shoes clunking on the rungs as he followed us.

William waited while I climbed the last ladder, which led to the main deck. "Don't you have your apprentice duties?" he asked as Charlie came into view.

"Tell me what you're going to do with Miss Maria," Charlie insisted.

My eyes met William's as he glanced up at me. "I'm going to escort her to the mess deck and make her some tea." He laughed. "Why, do you think you can make a better pot of tea than I can, lad?"

I continued up, stepping out onto the main deck right in front of Captain Foster.

"Good day, Maria," he said. "Where is McGregor?"

"William?" I asked uncertainly and he gave a curt nod. I pointed down the ladder I'd just left, hearing the sounds of climbing.

William's head appeared, followed by the rest of him. "What's wrong, lass? Captain." He and the captain exchanged nods as I looked from one to the other.

"I thought you were taking care of the girl, McGregor. Maybe I should assign the boy to her instead. Why did I hear her screaming below decks?"

"I don't know," William began.

"Fire," I said firmly. "Fear…fire."

Charlie tumbled to the deck at my feet, breathing hard. "Miss Maria was afraid of the fires in the boiler room. I made a joke that it looked like hell in there and Miss Maria believed me, sir. Mr McGregor –"

"The engine room is no place for a woman!" Captain Foster exploded, glaring at Charlie and William. He pointed at Charlie. "You should be hard at work or you'll never be anything but an apprentice. Get below." He turned to William. "I don't want her wandering around below decks. It's dangerous." His eyes flicked to me and I saw fear in them. "For a woman to be alone in places like that. Don't let her out of your sight and keep to the main decks. I don't want her near the engine room again. You should get her safely back to her cabin."

Charlie turned and headed back down the ladder, glaring balefully at all of us. He seemed to reserve extra anger for William as the man's arm came to rest around my shoulders. "First, we're going to the mess deck for a cup of tea to settle her nerves. I want to try and ask her about what happened to her and I was hoping…" William coughed. "Have you heard anything over the wireless about her vessel?

The one that was wrecked?"

Captain Foster shook his head. "I radioed to tell them about finding the wreckage she was floating on, but no one has word that any vessel has been lost in the storms. I haven't mentioned her because we might be ordered to return to Fremantle instead of heading to Durban as scheduled, so I want to wait until we're more than halfway. We have a better chance of finding an interpreter who understands her language there than in Australia, too. Anything you can find out about who she is and what she's doing out here...tell Allchin he can use my private stores if it'll help."

To my surprise, William winked at me as he took my arm. "There's an offer I don't need to hear twice. C'mon, lass, before he reconsiders. Have you ever tasted chocolate before? Chocolate?"

I stared at him, my feet moving automatically to keep pace with the hurrying man. What in the world was chocolate?

55

# Eight

The mess deck was empty but for Allchin and a small, dark-haired man that I didn't know. William said something to Allchin in a voice so low I didn't hear the words, but the cook nodded and disappeared into the kitchen.

The small man and William bowed their heads to one another, much like my people did. "MacuGuregoru-san," the man said.

William responded, "Kaito-san." He glanced at me. "This is Maria. Maria, Kaito-san is from Japan."

Kaito inclined his head. "*Hajimemashite*, Maria-san."

I smiled uncertainly and ducked my head. "Ha…hajimmy…" I looked to William, lost. I couldn't pronounce what Kaito had said, nor did I understand it.

"He said he's pleased to meet you, lass, or at least I think that's what he said. He might have asked about your health." William shrugged. "It's been a long time since I spoke any Japanese."

Kaito smiled. "It means both. Would you and Maria-san like to join me for tea?" He poured hot water from the kettle into a squat, shiny teapot. A wisp of steam curled up from the dark liquid.

I inhaled, then took another, deeper breath. The scent hit the back of my throat and transported me home. For a moment, I'd just finished a meal with my mother and sister. The brief flash of memory was so clear, but over so fast that tears sprang to my eyes. I'd never share a meal with either of them, ever again. I opened my eyes to find both men staring at me. The smell had strengthened and it was coming from Kaito's teapot.

"You like my tea, Maria-san?"

"Yes," I breathed. Surely the liquid wasn't the same brown stuff that William had given me. Each murky cup had looked and smelled like stewed seaweed and wet wood.

Kaito's smile didn't fade as he poured two cups of the fragrant tea. His teapot hovered over a third, empty cup. "MacuGuregoru-san?"

"No, I'll take my tea like we do at home." William lifted the large, brown teapot that dwarfed Kaito's black lacquered one, and poured his own tea. It was the darkest I'd ever seen it – or perhaps it was just in contrast to the fresh green of my drink. A splash of milk turned dark brown to tan, but it didn't attract me in the slightest.

"Maria-san," Kaito said, lifting his cup in salute. William did the same, as if this were some sort of ritual I didn't understand. Both drank together and I lifted my cup to do the same. The flavour was stronger than the smell and memory slugged me again, but I managed to control it this time as I sank onto a bench to cover my preoccupation with the past.

William sat across from me, slurping his tea with a smile pasted on his face.

The ship lurched beneath us and I grabbed the table to stop myself from slipping off the bench.

"Where did you learn Japanese, MacuGuregoru-san?" Kaito asked, his face paling as he sipped.

William appeared surprised at the question. "One of my friends at university was half Japanese. He was a champion boxer, but he'd learned to fight in some ancient Japanese style and he wanted to continue to practice. I was the only one who'd beaten him in the ring — once! — so I offered to learn. We studied together for four years and I learned some

Japanese when he couldn't remember the words in English. Bad juju fighting, the other boys called it, for it made me a better fighter." He took a deep draught of tea, which threatened to spill as the ship continued to move. "Or a worse one, if the boy was my opponent!"

Kaito smiled. "Did your friend study jujitsu in Japan? I would be interested in training with you some time. My father insisted I practice samurai hand-to-hand fighting every morning before breakfast and I fear I will forget his teachings if I don't continue to practice diligently." He ducked his head and I saw his knuckles whiten as he clung to the bench beneath him as if his life depended on it. "MacuGuregoru-san, Maria-san, please excuse me. My tea is yours." His hand shoved the teapot toward me before he staggered out of the door. His face was a delicate shade of green as he braced himself along the corridor and out of sight.

The ship was indeed moving more in the

swell – there were waves within my cup when I set it on the table. Grateful for Kaito's gift, I poured more green tea for myself and took a moment to savour the smell.

"Stewed grass," William said, nodding at my cup. "I don't know how you can drink that stuff. It even turned Kaito green, though the ship rolling's usually enough to do that to me – no strange drink necessary. Maybe I'm getting my sea legs after all. A bit bloody late, but better late than never."

William's unsettled stomach didn't seem to bother him any more, I reflected, noting that he happily drank his foul brew without any sign of the distress Kaito suffered from the ship's motion.

"You're in luck!" Allchin said, hurrying across the deck as if the swell didn't bother him in the slightest. "I found a whole box of the stuff, but it took me some time to find it. It says Plaistowe's British chocolate on the outside, but it's not a name or a sweet I've ever heard of. Must be some strange colonial imitation of the Cadbury's back home. Untouched until now, so I brought you two bars." He set a tin plate on the table, adorned with two long, brown blocks of something. "I found a good bottle of rum, too. I thought we were out before we hit the Panama Canal, but it turned out there was one left behind the condensed milk. No idea why the captain would order so much of the stuff."

William glanced at me. "Keep the rum in reserve – and out of sight. You never know when you might need it for medicinal purposes."

Allchin grinned and winked. "I think I just might." He disappeared into the kitchen.

William's full attention turned to me. "Now, lass. You never did answer before. Have you eaten chocolate?" He waved at the brown bars.

"Chocolate," I repeated slowly, then shook my head and pressed my lips together. If this tasted like his tea, I wasn't touching it.

He laughed and leaned forward with a

wicked smile on his face. "Maria, you are going to love me for the rest of your life for this. For a woman, I've heard it's better than the first time you…" He reddened and I wondered why. "Now, open your mouth."

I stared at him, mystified.

"Open your mouth, lass," he repeated, dropping his voice to a seductive purr. I may not have understood his words, but his tone brought a smile to my lips. He leaned closer, so that his deep ocean eyes bored into mine. His lips parted and so did mine, to draw a shaky breath into my suddenly dry mouth. I wanted to kiss this man, whose lips were but a breath away.

His finger grazed my lower lip as he slipped it inside my mouth. No, not his finger — a cold piece of the brown material, which he left on my tongue. His fingers pushed my chin up so that I closed my mouth on the morsel.

I closed my eyes, breathing deeply as I resisted the urge for violence that bubbled up.

How dare he deny me the kiss he'd been so keen to give me, replacing his warm tongue with the cold substance I didn't want. The stuff was melting on my tongue, much like the butter he'd spread on my toast that morning. The first taste was bitter and I drew myself up to spit the offending object at his face.

"Wait, please," he implored, pressing his index finger over my lips as if he wished to hush me.

Buttery bitterness melted and sweetness filled my mouth like nothing I'd ever tasted before. My eyes flew open in surprise as the smooth confection slid down my throat. William's grin told me he knew exactly what I was thinking as he popped a piece of chocolate into his own mouth. He chewed it and broke off another piece. "More?"

"Oh yes," I breathed.

Together, we finished off both of the blissful bars before William's hands closed over mine on the table. "Maria, I need to know what happened to you. When you were afraid in the boiler room…was it because you've seen a ship on fire before? You feared this ship was on fire, too?"

I tried to summon the words. "Ship…fire. Dead men. Burning." The memory was still painfully clear. How much time must pass before it would fade?

He squeezed my hands. "You must have been terrified. A ship on fire, alone at sea, is a fearful thing. How did you escape?" My bewilderment must have showed, because he tried again. "You're not dead on the fiery ship. Not burned. Alive – how?"

I pulled my hands out of his and tried to show him.

His arms mirrored the arcs mine made. "You dived into the water and swam away?"

I circled my hands uncertainly. "Swim? Swim…ocean."

"What about sharks? Weren't you afraid of sharks? Or weren't there any?" he pressed.

"Sharks, yes," I began uncertainly. "No fear. Big fish." I held up a fist and feinted a punch in front of him. "Sharks…fear." My smile died on my lips at William's shock.

"You leaped off a burning ship into shark-infested waters and fought them off?" He shook his head in disbelief. "Maria, that's crazy. You can't possibly have…what was the ship's name?"

"Name…ship?" I repeated.

He nodded. "Yes. What was the name of the burning ship?"

I wet my lips. "*Emden.*"

His brow furrowed. "I've heard that name before. It was a warship…a big victory for the British during the war. You can't have come from that. They only allow men on warships and anyway, it was sunk years ago at some island in the Indian Ocean. Here. It was sunk off some colony here!" He stared at me. "You're the daughter of some rich colonist out here, aren't you? Or…you're his wife." His eyes held hurt. "That's why you didn't scream like my sister or any normal girl would when you saw Charlie naked. You're not an innocent at all. You're a married woman. Married and…your husband will be looking for you. Combing the whole damn ocean in search of you, I bet."

From the warm, admiring man, he'd suddenly turned cold and distant. It was the name of the ship. It had to be. He knew what I'd done.

William's hands cupped my face, his sad eyes holding mine. "His name. Maria, tell me his name so I can help you return to his arms." He wiped my tears away with his fingers. "His name or the name of his ship. I'll find him and I swear I'll see you safely home to him."

"Giuseppe," I whispered, the tears flowing faster still. I tried to illustrate my words with my hands, in the faint hope that he'd understand. "Ship…sank and sharks…Giuseppe no swim. Sank. Sharks. Sharks…dead. Giuseppe dead." I laid my head on the table and sobbed. He was the only man I'd ever loved and the ocean took him away from me.

I felt the bench jump as William's weight landed beside me. Warm arms enveloped me, pulling me to his chest. "I'm sorry, lass. Not a wife – a widow and a newly bereaved one, at that. I'm so sorry. If I'd known, I wouldn't have pushed so hard. No wonder you didn't want to talk about it. To see the man you love drown and have to survive at sea, all on your own…I don't know a single woman who'd be brave enough to do what you did."

His unfamiliar words washed over me, but I could still hear his warm tone as he stroked my hair, holding me tight. My heart beat faster at each caress. Giuseppe was no longer the only man I'd ever loved. I was fast falling for someone else. I knew that if any man could mend my broken heart, it was William.

# Nine

An ear-splitting noise woke me. For a moment, I was terrified – it sounded like the same blaring horn that called the crew to combat on warships. I'd seen enough of such battles to last a lifetime. The only thing louder than the call to arms in my memory were the screams of the dying – far too many for me to count.

I'd go over the side, into the water, before I'd witness another naval battle.

"Time to get dressed up and go for a walk,

lass." William's voice was surprisingly calm. He grinned as he grabbed a towel to dry his freshly-washed face.

Why did the prospect of war make him so cheerful?

He hung the towel over the rail and turned to face me. Something saddened him and his voice turned soft and coaxing. "It's all right, Maria. I'm sure it's only another drill – the captain swears the regular drills while he was in the Royal Navy saved his life. Don't worry. I'll take care of you. Now, get down here before the captain comes looking for us. If the ship really is sinking, we don't want to be slow."

William held out his hands and I took them, sliding from the bunk to thump feet-first onto the deck. He led me out of the cabin, as unhurried as if we were headed to breakfast, but he bypassed the deserted mess hall. I wasn't sure where or why he was taking me, but my instincts told me to trust him. He'd had three days and two nights to attack me, if that was his desire. Of course he'd touched me, but, like his tone, he kept all contact between us both courteous and gentle. He hadn't even pulled my hair when he'd combed it.

The wind hit me as we reached the main deck – a cold air current that made me turn my face to it, closing my eyes and breathing deep to savour the freshness. It plastered my shirt against my chest and turned my nipples into hard chips of ice. Oh, how I loved it.

"Here. Take it, lass, before you freeze."

I felt something rough and gritty brush my arm, and opened my eyes. William held out his salt-encrusted, woollen jumper with an entreating look on his face. He clenched his other arm against his body, as if the wind chilled him more than it did me. I shook my head, laughing as I pushed the jumper away. I wanted as little as possible between me and the bracing breeze.

Reluctantly, he pulled it back over his head and grasped my hand again. He led me along the deck to a spot out of the wind. A crewman stood beside a large, open box, handing out canvas pillows with trailing ribbons. He already had one tied around his torso.

"Have you ever worn a lifejacket, lass?" William asked, pressing the surprisingly hard pillow against my chest. He helped me pull the awkward thing over my head before he tied the ribbons securely around me. When he was similarly trussed, he led me through a maze of boxes and crates and along the path that skirted the deck.

I scanned the grey-green waters, searching for the other ships that had provoked the call to arms, but I saw nothing but us, clear to the horizon. Turning to survey the sea in the other direction, I bumped into something hard. I squeezed my eyes shut at the blinding pain in my head.

William's warm fingers touched my forehead. "Ooh, that was a nasty bump. You should watch where you're going — these lifeboats could save your life. You don't want to dent one with that hard head of yours." For a moment, the only sound was wind and that blaring horn, before he continued, "Are you all right? Do you want to lie down? I'll carry you back to the cabin when we're done, but we have to wait here until the whole crew's assembled."

I forced my eyes open. The stars had faded and the initial, shocking pain, too. The dull ache it left behind was bearable. I turned my eyes on the object I'd collided with – a small, wooden boat suspended at head height to catch the unwary. Another hung behind it and two more mirrored these on the starboard side of the vessel.

I lost interest in the boats as I realised the whole crew was standing on the deck and they all seemed to be staring at us.

"If you're this slow in a real crisis, McGregor, the lifeboats might launch without you, leaving you to your fate," Captain Foster said.

"You wouldn't leave without us, captain,"

William replied. "The sound of the alarm horns terrified Maria. You could have given the poor girl some warning. After the ordeal she's been through, it seems hardly fair to scare her into thinking this ship's sinking, too."

Captain Foster's expression hardened. "Just because a ship rescues you once, doesn't mean it's safe. I learned that in the Atlantic. Those German U-boats had it in for me that day. Maria!"

I jumped at the sound of my name, but my eyes were already on the angry captain.

"When you hear that sound, it means the ship's sinking and if you don't hurry, you'll sink with her and drown. Do you understand?" I stared at the man, mystified at what I'd done to make him look so desperate. He stomped his foot on the deck and waved his hands. "The ship. Tell me you know what a ship is!"

I wet my lips and pointed at the deck beneath my feet. "Ship," I said slowly.

"Hallelujah, she's not as stupid as we

thought," a voice sneered and several men laughed.

Painstakingly, Captain Foster lifted one hand and rippled it like the swell beneath the ship. "Ocean." I nodded – this word I knew. He floated his other hand above the first. "Ship." I nodded again. His ship hand took a sudden dive, plunging down beneath the surface of his make-believe ocean. "Ship sinking."

"Ship sinking," I repeated warily, wondering what he knew of such things. Surely this ship wasn't…please, no! I raced to the rail, leaning over to stare at the waves. The ship didn't look any lower in the water than it usually did. I stormed back to the captain. "NO ship sinking."

William burst out laughing. "She's got you there, captain. You did scare the life out of her this morning for no good reason. I think we'd all be in for a tongue-lashing if she knew enough English. Thank God for small mercies."

Captain Foster's eyes bored into mine. "If the ship's sinking, that horn will blow." He stabbed a finger at the source of the blaring sound. "And you leg it up to the lifeboats if you want to live." He slapped the side of the nearest lifeboat with unnecessary force, making it rock in its davits. "That's it for today's drill. Get back to work." He wrenched his life jacket off and stalked to the box where they belonged.

Bewildered, I stood unmoving as a sea of men swept past me to follow the captain. William yanked my arm, pulling me behind the lifeboats to make way for the others to pass. He helped me remove my lifejacket and passed both of them to Charlie, who joined the queue of men waiting to return the bulky items to their box. The ship seemed eerily quiet when the siren ceased.

"Don't be afraid, lass," William said, lifting the cover on one of the boats. "These are much better than your flimsy raft and you survived on that. I heard stories of how shipwrecked Dutchmen and Englishmen have crossed this ocean in boats no bigger than our lifeboats – men who lived to find land. They didn't have the supplies ours do, either – and we can thank Captain Foster for that. He was cast into a boat just like these in the war and he survived. If our luck turns bad and we have to board these, I'L lift you aboard the captain's boat myself, for I know he'll steer us safely to land." He held out his arms. "Here, I'll help you up so you can take a look for yourself." I stepped closer and was surprised when his hands closed around my waist, lifting me into the air.

I panicked and caught the edge of the boat, swinging my legs up over the gunwale, and clumsily hooked my body into the craft. The plank seats stopped me from rolling to the bottom of the boat, but I had barely a second to catch my breath before the boat tipped dangerously and I had to cling to the bench to stop myself from falling out as William climbed over the side.

He dropped to his knees and wrenched open a locker beneath a bench. "Come and see." He gestured for me to come closer and I inched my way along the seat to look underneath it. William pulled a tin from the multitude crammed inside the locker and held it up. "Captain Foster's supplies. He refused to put to sea unless the lifeboats were stocked with as much condensed milk as water. He says he'll find a way to make it law – all lifeboats should carry condensed milk. One crazy Scotsman, trying to change the world." He laughed, but his eyes turned sad. "I didn't want to change it, only see it, but now I'm beginning to understand why my brothers wanted to settle down. Halfway round the world, in the middle of the ocean, and I finally see –"

"You planning on sailing away into the sunset with your little whore, McGregor? Is that what took you so long to appear on deck? You had to pull your cock out of her and get her clothes back on? Plenty of hard-working men on this ship — seems to me you should share, seeing as you're only a passenger and all." A hand caught my foot, almost yanking me out of the boat.

William grabbed me before I fell. "Leave the girl alone, Sciarra. You're lucky she doesn't understand a word of your filth — I'll let it go this time, but if you say it again, I'll break your face."

I twisted so I could see the grinning idiot behind me. I might not have understood his words, but I didn't like his tone, or his hands clutching at me.

"Go on, McGregor, just a taste," Sciarra wheedled, his tongue snaking toward my ankle.

Revolted, I kicked and felt the satisfying crunch as my feet met his face. He landed on his back on the deck. Shock morphed to fury on his face and he sprang to his feet. "You bitch…"

I shifted to a crouch, ready to leap out of the boat to tackle him to the deck, but William beat me to it, landing lightly on his feet between us. "Get the hell out of here, Sciarra, before I hurt you worse than she has."

I let myself down to the deck, glaring at the horrible man, his lip bleeding from the damage I'd inflicted. I itched to hit him again.

"Put a leash on her," Sciarra muttered as he stalked away.

William and I both stared after him until I felt his fingers close around mine. "I don't know what it is about you, but you drive men crazy with how much we want you. I know if you were mine, I'd never want to let you go." He squeezed my hand. "Even now, I don't want to." William laughed shakily as his eyes bored into mine. "Probably a good thing you don't understand me. If I'd said that to any of the girls back home, they'd be buying a wedding dress that very day. Maybe it's because I've never seen you in a dress. I wonder if I ever will." The wind swept away his laughter as he led me to the mess deck for breakfast.

I clasped his hand tightly in both of mine, shaken at the message in his eyes that he'd reinforced with words I'd understood. If this ship sank, I'd fight off sharks to see him safely to land. William wouldn't suffer Giuseppe's fate. "No let go," I murmured, but I doubt he heard.

# Ten

I swallowed the last bite of my sandwich and tried not to wish for food from home. Shipboard life was as dull as the food – I moved from cabin to mess and back again, seeing little else aside from glimpses of water and sky. It seemed almost too much effort to get up for more of the same.

A hand grabbed mine and yanked my arm, almost tipping me off the bench. William was instantly on his feet, his larger hand fastened over the skinny, offending wrist. "Let go of her, lad."

"I have a surprise for her, Mr McGregor," Charlie said. "Come on, you have to come out on deck." He jerked his head toward the door. "I want to show you something."

"I'm sure it can wait a couple of minutes so Maria can finish her meal. Have you eaten yet?" William released Charlie, but he didn't leave my side.

Charlie marched up to the counter and grabbed a sandwich in each hand. "I'll eat on deck," he insisted. "Come on. I don't want you to miss it." His eyes beseeched me.

I smiled and rose. Charlie grinned so widely, I thought his face would split. I followed him up to the bow, where the ship endlessly parted the waves.

"Have you ever seen anything like it, miss?" he asked, staring avidly at the bow wave, where the sunlight created rainbows in the spray.

I placed both hands on the rail and followed his gaze. A fin…no, more than one. A dolphin burst from the bow wave and flipped in the air, circling until it splashed back into the water. Two fins rose up in its place. I couldn't help laughing for joy. I'd never seen spinner dolphins from such a high vantage point before. I leaned over the rail, trying to count the swimming bodies keeping pace with the ship, but there were too many of them. More than a hundred. A pod this large could only be congregating for a reason. I peered into the depths, then lifted my eyes to the ocean in front of the ship. Did the sun catch on something, or was I imagining it?

"Careful, lass, or you'll find out how cold the Indian Ocean is in winter. As will I, for I'll dive in after you to fish you out again," William's voice said in my ear as he curled an arm around my waist.

"Aww, Mr McGregor, Maria's safe with me!" Charlie complained, aiming a bitter look at my protector. "I can protect her. I'm not afraid of a fight!"

"I'm sure you're right, lad, but she's my responsibility. And I wanted to see what could make her smile so brightly. Have you ever seen a dolphin before, Maria?"

"I know I've never seen so many. There must be at least ten of them!" Charlie insisted.

I shook my head, pointing. "More. Fish."

William laughed gently. "They're not fish, lass. They're dolphins — as warm-blooded as you or me."

Frustrated at not knowing the words, I shook my head harder. "No. Fish!"

As if to illustrate the point I'd failed to make, a cloud of flying fish rose from the water, followed by a dozen dolphins and a second, smaller wave of the marine mammals. A much-reduced cloud splashed down half a minute later.

Charlie burst out laughing. "She was right. The dolphins are fishing for flying fish. Was that how you survived on the raft? Did dolphins help you?"

William snorted. "They're just animals. The stories about them helping shipwrecked sailors are just that — stories."

"I heard that there are some places in the world where dolphins and fishermen work together to catch fish. Mr Kaito said…"

"Ohhh…no more fish," I said, pointing as the huge pod of spinner dolphins veered away from the ship. A younger one stayed with the bow wave for a little longer, turning in dizzying circles until it realised it was alone. It launched itself into the air in the wake of the rest of its community.

I watched the dolphins leaping and swimming off into the distance and I yearned for that kind of freedom. Today, sun glinted off the waves for the first time since I'd boarded this ship and it looked so pretty. The ocean matched William's eyes again, I decided, glancing from one to the other.

Something warm and clammy closed over my fingers, pressing them against the railing. Charlie's hand. He stared in the direction of the dolphins, his body stiffened by the same nervous energy that had made his palms sweaty. I realised that the boy cherished romantic or at least lustful hopes for me – something my broken heart could never return. I leaned closer and kissed Charlie's cheek, feeling William's arm tighten around me. "Thank you, Charlie."

Charlie turned pink. "Y-you're welcome, mmm-Miss Maria," he managed to say.

A whistle sounded behind us. "It just keeps getting better and better! The girl with the big tits is a whore who does two at the same time. What d'you say, Barrett? Fancy a tumble with this one? Seeing as we saved her life, the first time should be free."

Charlie jumped away from me. "She's not a…how dare you say that about…" he spluttered.

With William close behind me, we turned together, but he dropped his arm so that he no longer held me.

Two men stood on the deck – Barrett and Sciarra – and both leered at me with unmistakeable lust. Lust they wouldn't slake anywhere near me, I swore. Rage rose up inside me — far hotter than the anger that turned Charlie's face red. The day either of these men touched me would be the day they died. And I wanted that to be today.

I took a step toward them before William grabbed me, both arms cinching around my waist. "No, lass, that's what they want. They want to hurt you."

I wasn't sure that I could take out the unpleasant men without harming William or Charlie — and William knew his people and these men better than I did. I let him restrain me for a moment. A slight delay didn't matter — after all, these men were trapped on this ship with me until we made port. I had plenty of time.

"Apologise to the lady," William demanded. "Or I'll see that you regret it."

"That's a whore. No lady," Barrett spat.

"The next time you spit, I promise you it'll be blood and your own teeth, you rude bastard son of a whore." William replied before lowering his voice to add, "Beg pardon,

Maria."

"You might be able to take him, McGregor, but you're no match for me. I'll wager a night with your whore on the fight. You win, you keep her. I win, I get her all to myself." Sciarra's grin glittered with malice.

William's arms tightened around my waist. "I've never lost a fight. By the time I'm finished with you, you won't be able to talk at all, let alone insult ladies. Your own mother won't recognise your face when I'm done. When I've beaten both of you so you're lying on the deck, crying like little girls, you'll leave the lady alone."

"He fought off six of the Queen's men. They lived because one coward pulled a gun and shot him. You're the girl, McGregor, and the whore is ours."

Both William and Charlie burst out laughing, but it was Charlie who cried, "You mean the poxy whore queen of Sydney? Queen of the night or the underworld or whatever they call her? I heard it was six of her whores you fought, not men, and you pissed and shat yourself before she shot you for trying to sneak out without paying. Mr McGregor will pound you into the deck!"

"Tomorrow, after our shift ends," Sciarra said with a nod to Barrett. "And I'll be first, so while you're lying on the deck in a pool of your own blood and Barrett's kicking three kinds of shit out of you, I'll be fucking your little girlfriend."

The two men sauntered off toward the stern, the smoke from their cigarettes drifting up in their wake.

"You'll win, won't you, Mr McGregor? You can't let them hurt Maria. It's just not right…" Charlie said, turning desperate eyes toward William.

William released me and I spun so I could see his worried face. "Of course, lad. Now, I think I should get Maria below, before that cloudburst hits." He nodded toward the dark cloud bearing down on us. "Winter in the Indian Ocean. It makes me miss Scotland's storms."

# Eleven

The following morning, William seemed intent on showing me how to move furniture. "While I'm gone, you keep this door shut and push the locker in front of it. Wedge it against the bunk like this if you can." He moved the locker so that it was jammed between the door and the bunk, trapping us inside. As afternoon approached, he seemed more and more worried and he stopped speaking. Instead, he balled his hands into fists and punched the air at an imaginary opponent — first on one side of him, then the other. After the verbal altercation yesterday, he seemed to be preparing for a fight with the two men. I hoped it wouldn't come to that.

He didn't eat a bite at lunch. He just stared at me, grinding his teeth against each other in the absence of food, until I'd finished eating. Then, without saying a word, he took my arm and marched me back to our cabin.

"As soon as I'm gone, I want you to barricade this door. Don't let anyone in. Do you understand me?"

I looked into his worried eyes and nodded, hoping that was the response he required. I wished I understood.

This seemed to satisfy him. He leaned down and pressed his lips to my forehead. "Don't worry, lass. I won't lose and I'll be back. The crew will leave you alone after I deal with these two. Just don't let anyone in until I come back."

My forehead still felt warm from his touch

as I watched him hurry out of the cabin, clanging the door shut behind him.

I looked at the locker on the floor by the door and sighed. I started hauling it back to its place beneath the porthole, wishing I knew why William had wanted me to imprison myself alone in this tiny room.

I gave the locker one last shove and heard frenzied hammering on the cabin door. The door flew open and Charlie burst in, breathless and flushed. "Miss! Maria! It's time. Come quickly!" He grabbed my arm and tugged.

Mystified, I allowed the excited boy to pull me down the corridor and up the ladder to the main deck.

"It's Mr McGregor! He's fighting for your honour, like some sort of knight in a fairy tale!" He led me to the stern, down another ladder to where crates and barrels were stacked.

I heard the rumble of voices and the smack of flesh on flesh before I saw them, but I knew what I'd find. William hadn't been dreading trouble – he'd made an appointment with it. We rounded a stack of barrels and I almost bumped into two men who were waving their fists in the air, urging someone on.

Charlie pushed and jumped, but he couldn't push through the milling crowd which looked like it consisted of the majority of the crew. He looked around and pointed. "The mast, miss. We'll have a good view from the mast. Do you think you can climb a rope ladder? I can help you if you want." He hurried to the mast and gestured. "You go first, miss. I'll climb below you so I can catch you if you fall."

The tarred hemp was rough and sticky beneath my hands and feet, swaying in the stiff breeze, but I clambered up the rope ladder quickly, curling my toes around the beam at the top as I hugged the mast for support. I could see the combatants now and I couldn't tear my eyes away.

Stripped down to their trousers, both men circled each other in the clear patch of deck that was marked off by a rope draped around barrels and crates, creating a rough ring. The rest of the crew crowded around the rope fence, pumping their fists and shouting insults or encouragement – it was hard to tell which, or who it was directed at. The sound was angry and primal.

One man's fist cracked against the other's chin, followed by his other fist smashing the man's nose. Blood spurted, streaming down the man's face and onto his bare chest.

"Yeah, Mr McGregor! You show him what happens when you say bad things about Miss Maria!" Charlie hooted beside me.

Startled, William turned his head to stare at Charlie before his gaze shifted to me. I saw pain in his eyes and I felt responsible. No man should hurt for me when all he'd done was help me. He hadn't wanted me to see this.

"NO!" I gasped as the bloody-faced man took advantage of William's distraction to take a swing at him. William dodged, but the blow still landed, splitting his lip.

"Yeah, go, Barrett! Beat him good!" A single cheer rose up from a man with two black eyes – one of them swollen shut and bleeding. I recognised the man sitting in a puddle as Sciarra and my hands tightened on the mast, wishing I could wrap them around the man's throat.

I watched William wipe a trickle of blood from his chin as he advanced on Barrett. He delivered a series of jabs to the man's midsection and I heard the crack of breaking bone. Barrett stumbled back, but William pursued him, punching him in the face repeatedly. Barrett seemed to have trouble breathing, but somehow he remained on his feet. He said something I couldn't hear and spat in William's face. William's final blow smacked into the side of the man's head, spinning him around before Barrett collapsed on the deck. The crowd fell silent.

William pulled a handkerchief from his pocket and wiped his face.

Someone grabbed Barrett's legs and dragged him out of the makeshift ring. I watched in satisfaction as someone splashed a bucket of seawater over his face to rouse him and he came up spluttering. Shoving the man with the bucket out of his way, Barrett stormed toward the bow, taking the rungs of the ladder two at a time.

William drank a cup of water and rinsed his mouth. He threw the cup down and held his arms out in an angry invitation, saying, "Who's next? Anyone else want to challenge me?"

A slim, black-haired man slipped under the rope to stand in the ring and I gasped as I recognised the polite green tea drinker. "I'll be your opponent."

Both men gave each other a short nod, as if accepting the other's challenge.

The surrounding crew seemed to think this was a signal to start arguing and exchanging pieces of paper. None of them looked happy.

"Betting on the outcome, miss. Mr

McGregor's beaten every man he's ever fought, but so has Mr Kaito. No one's game to fight Mr Kaito, but sometimes they're brave enough to challenge Mr McGregor."

"You'll need to let go of your anger if you wish to beat me, MacuGuregoru-san," Kaito said with an eerie smile.

"Save your breath, Kaito," William replied, squaring up his fists for another bout. The crowd hushed.

The two men circled, throwing and dodging punches in a mesmerising dance. Without the blood or the blows, it was hard to believe the men were combatants. I could hear their bare feet shuffling against the boards, it was so quiet.

I held my breath. There was something about this dance that seemed far more dangerous than William's bout with Barrett. Perhaps it was the calm smile on Kaito's face.

Kaito's arm lifted, then jerked down in a chopping motion toward William's neck. To my surprise, William caught the blow with his forearm. Kaito's smile widened. I could barely keep track of the flurry of blows that followed, as both seemed to want to hit the other with the sides of their hand as well as closed fists, and each blocked the other by mirroring their attack.

They circled again, exchanging blows and blocks as the crowd started to murmur. Kaito lifted his leg to kick and I gasped as William blocked that, too. The dance intensified as the two men attacked one another with both arms and feet. I'd never seen anything like it and neither had the hushed crowd. Kaito caught William's kick in his hands and both men spun apart. William was panting, but he didn't take his eyes off his opponent.

"Showing off for the lady. What will happen to her if you're defeated, MacuGuregoru-san?"

William charged at Kaito and the fight began again. This time, William landed first one blow, then another, on the other man's ribs, but Kaito delivered a crunching kick to

William's diaphragm that evened the score. While William wheezed for breath, Kaito tenderly touched what I hoped were broken ribs. As if he'd read my thoughts, the Japanese man lifted his gaze to me.

"What is the girl thinking as she watches her protector lose to his own anger, MacuGuregoru-san?" he said softly.

"No," I whispered as William charged Kaito again. Kaito somehow flipped William from his feet to his back, so William lay gasping on the deck, still struggling to breathe.

The crowd seemed to be waiting for something before Kaito held his fist in the air and they cheered.

"Who will challenge me?" he called.

William clambered onto his hands and knees. "I'm not finished yet," he croaked. He crawled over to a barrel and used it to hoist himself to his feet. "I won't lose to you, you cold bastard." He lifted his arms into a fighting stance, but it looked like one breath would tip him over again.

"You have courage, MacuGuregoru-san, but you should surrender now. It is no dishonour among your people."

Kaito's tight smile set me on edge. I didn't understand his words, but it sounded like sneering to me – a deliberate taunt to make William attack him and face more pain and humiliation. I would not permit it.

Balancing on the balls of my feet, I leaped from my high perch, feeling the rush of air as I dropped toward the deck. I tucked my body into a ball just before I hit, rolling with the impact so that I could jump to my feet between them. I'd judged the distance almost perfectly – I could feel the heat of William's panting breath on my neck as I saw the fear in Kaito's eyes.

William's arm closed around my waist as he tried to pull me back. "A boxing ring is no place for a lady, Maria. You shouldn't be here. Too…dangerous."

Kaito stepped back cautiously, his eyes never leaving mine. "Among my people, there are stories of women samurai, MacuGuregoru-san – warriors who all men feared. This one may have the soul of such a warrior."

He feinted at me and I dodged, shaking free of William's restraining arms. I might not have their experience in inflicting violence, but that didn't make me helpless.

The next blow he aimed was no feint, but it didn't connect, either. He moved and I darted away, the tiniest twinge of his muscles telling me which way to go. He started slow, but my smile only widened as I turned, ducked, dodged and stepped out of his reach. Blows rained harder and faster, but I kept up, twisting my body as I danced away from the man. I was lighter on my feet and it showed – I was always a step ahead of him.

I saw a twitch in his thigh as he aimed a kick at me and I leaped, twisting in mid-air to avoid a well-placed fist as his leg swept beneath me. As our dance picked up the tempo, I couldn't wipe the smile from my face – even in my cumbersome clothing, I'd never felt so free. Wanting to see how he'd floored William so quickly, I advanced on him as if I wished to attack.

His eyes flashed in triumph as he seized my lapel with one hand and the waistband of my pants with the other. His foot hooked behind my knee, pulling me toward him, and I tipped back, lowered to the deck by his grip on my clothing. The moment he released me, I rolled, rising to my feet.

"McGregor! I said if there was any more fighting on my ship I'd drop the culprit overboard. I don't care if you're a paying passenger and my wife's cousin, by God I'll send you off in a lifeboat with naught but yourself for company if I find you fighting again." The crowd eddied aside, as if a strong rip pulled everything out of its path.

Kaito's attention was riveted on the shouting captain's approach, along with everyone else.

"McGregor! Do you want the girl to think we're a pack of savages, beating the daylights out of each other until they fall to the deck?"

I swallowed and tried to remember the sequence. Shoulder, hip, hook, pull…oh, my. Kaito smacked to the deck, looking shocked as he stared up at me. I burst out laughing.

"What the deuce is going on here?" Captain Foster demanded.

William coughed. "It started as a friendly competition, captain. A few men challenged me to a boxing match and we placed some small wagers. Others came to watch and I won the first few bouts, before Kaito beat me to become the next champion."

"An amateur boxing match is hardly the place for a woman, McGregor." Captain Foster glanced at me, then glared back at William.

William looked like he was trying not to laugh. "So I said to her, captain. Only Maria…I don't think she agreed with me. Then she…she dropped Kaito here to the deck." He offered his arm to the man and Kaito took it, rising to his feet.

Now all eyes were on me.

"This girl beat a man in a boxing ring?" Captain Foster's voice dripped with the disbelief reflected in his wide eyes. I lifted my chin to meet his gaze. I didn't fear this man, but I began to believe that he feared me more than a little.

Both William and Kaito nodded. "It seems she knows a bit of his Eastern hand-to-hand fighting, too."

Captain Foster didn't seem to know what to do. Turning away from me, his shoulders sagged. "I want everyone to get back on duty. And you, McGregor – get her out of my sight. If the shipowners knew I'd let a woman get into a boxing match with the crew…they'd be outraged. Take her below – looks like we have another storm coming in."

William grabbed his shirt off the top of the crate and curled an arm around my shoulders.

"Better do what he says, lass. You don't want to be stuck in a lifeboat on your lonesome again, I'm sure."

# Twelve

William slammed the door behind us and threw his shirt on his bunk. "What were you thinking? Why didn't you stay here like I told you to?" he demanded, lifting the bucket of water onto the locker. He cupped some water in his hands and splashed it on his face before he dumped the remainder over his head, sending water everywhere – even on me, on the other side of the tiny cabin. A puddle started to form on the deck by his feet. "A fight is no place for a woman. You could have been…ungh!" His words faded into agonised sounds as he gingerly fingered his ribs. Bruises were already forming beneath the skin and I feared the bones were broken.

He dropped to his knees and rummaged through the locker. Pulling out a roll of cloth, he held it out to me. "Here. All women know how to bandage, don't they? Natural-born nurses and all."

I took the roll and examined it. It was barely bigger than my fist – a rolled strip perhaps as wide as my wrist. I stared at the man who now stood before me. He looked expectant, but I lifted my shoulders in a shrug. I had no idea what he wanted me to do.

He made an exasperated sound and snatched the cloth back. William proceeded to unroll the fabric, wrapping it around his chest repeatedly, grimacing in pain as the poorly-applied bandage slipped down his torso.

Realisation dawned. He wanted me to bind his broken ribs. "William," I said, reaching out to touch him. The bandage slipped from his fingers and slid down to his waist. I smiled as I unwound it. First, I needed to check where he was injured – if I put too much pressure on a different injury to support his ribs, I could do further damage.

I touched my fingers to the darkest bruising.

"Hey! That hurts!" he complained, shrinking away from my touch.

Holding my hand over his injury, I repeated, "Hurts?" I shifted my hand to his stomach, which appeared undamaged. "No hurts?" For what felt like the hundredth time, I wished I knew the words to ask him for what I needed. I wanted to be able to say, "Tell me what hurts, you great big baby, so I know what to tend first."

William sighed and pointed to his bruise. "This hurts." He gestured at his cheek, where his angry scrubbing had reopened the cut on his lip. "This." He held up his hands, so that I could see where the skin had split across his reddened knuckles. "These, too."

I nodded, but it was his ribs that I focussed

on. Broken or just bruised? Kaito had kicked him hard, but surely not hard enough to break bone, nor had William crashed into anything afterwards. Avoiding the dark discolouration, I probed the hard muscle around it. His skin was hot and moist beneath my fingers, but he didn't flinch the way he had before. Trying to be as light as possible, I touched the bruising again, following the line of his ribs to ascertain if there really was a fracture. No – they seemed intact.

"No broke. Hurt, no broke," I announced, biting the unravelled cloth to tear it into two pieces. I took his hand in mine and bound his fingers in the length of cloth, tying it at the end to secure it. I did the same with his other hand. "No hurt," I assured him, smiling.

His lips lifted a little and blood trickled from the cut. I had no cloth left, but I knew where he kept his handkerchief. I slipped my fingers into his pants pocket, feeling for the folded square of fabric. Through the thin pocket lining, I could feel more hot, hard muscle beneath, but I'd also found the bunched-up handkerchief, so I withdrew my hand and dabbed at his lip. William took the handkerchief from me and did his own dabbing, looking conflicted.

"You shouldn't go rifling through a man's pockets like that. You might find things a lady like yourself shouldn't…oughtn't…" He stopped as if searching for the words to continue while his face grew red with embarrassment. This seemed to fuel some fire within him. "What were you thinking? Jumping from the mast into a ring of fighting men. You could have been killed. You could have been hurt. One of them might have attacked you – I might have attacked you. Kaito did. Did he hit you – hurt you?" Anger turned to panic. "Are you hurt?" He framed my face in his hands, his eyes boring into mine.

I shook my head. I might not understand all of his words, but his body and his voice spoke volumes to me. While his voice was angry, his eyes were concerned, with the edge of panic that permeated his words at the end. Not to mention the tender way his hands held me now. My wellbeing mattered to him. I mattered to him. A smile lifted my lips as I said, "No, William. No hurt."

"Good," he murmured, pressing his lips to mine. His warm kiss swept me away on a thrilling wave that bubbled through my body like sea-foam. His tongue surged into my mouth and I tightened my arms around his neck, though I couldn't recall how they'd found their way to what felt like the most natural place for them to be.

"Oh, William," I sighed when we paused for breath. My lips tingled from his kisses and the bristly hair on his upper lip and chin. His fingers combed through my hair as I rested my head against his. I never wanted to let him go.

The bell-like clanging of someone hitting the door startled me. William gently disengaged from me as the door swung open and Charlie staggered inside, holding a bottle in one hand. "Mr Allchin bet against you in the fight. He lost so much money that he offered me rum instead. I took it and I thought I should share it with you and Maria, seeing as you two won me the bottle…hic!" He wove through the tiny cabin until he bumped against the wall and stood there with a bemused smile on his face.

William took the bottle from his hand. "You should eat something before you drink too much more of that, boy. How about we leave it here and go see what we can find in the mess." He set the bottle down and ushered both of us out of the cabin.

The mess deck was half-full, but all conversation died when we entered. No one seemed willing to meet my eyes – they were all very intent on the unappetising food. William noticed my unease and all three of us finished our food in record time, not lingering to talk.

When we returned to our cabin, William pulled me aside as Charlie went in. "You should head up to your bunk. Out of reach – just to be safe," William whispered to me, indicating that I should ascend. A glance at Charlie, who was clumsily swigging from the rum bottle, told me the boy wasn't entirely in control of his body any more, so I clambered up the ladder and sat cross-legged on my bunk. My head almost brushed the low ceiling.

Charlie held out the bottle. "To old-fashioned chivalry and lovely ladies!" he shouted, lifting the bottle to his lips. He stopped drinking abruptly and started coughing, then wiped his mouth and handed the bottle to William.

"I'll drink to the lady," William said, taking a swig. He stared at the label. "That's not a bad bottle of rum. I bet Allchin was saving that. Maria, would you like a taste?" He lifted the rum and I stretched for it, snagging the bottle from his hand.

Both men stared at me as I brought the open mouth to my lips. The liquor had a strong smell that burned my nose and my throat, I found as I swallowed a large mouthful of the stuff. Cautiously, I took another, smaller sip, but it was no less fiery. If anything, it stoked the flames in my throat even higher. I held the bottle out to the men – I wasn't sure I wanted any more.

Someone took it from me – I didn't notice who, as I was preoccupied with the effect the drink had on my body. The burning sensation spread from my throat outwards, diffusing into a warm, pleasant buzz. I gasped, focussing purely on the feeling. The only time I'd ever felt anything like this was in Giuseppe's arms – or when I'd kissed William though the bottled warmth was far inferior to both of these. It was like comparing my raft to this ship. No comparison at all, really.

After several minutes, I became accustomed to the rum's effects and I thought about tasting it once more. I crept forward, my legs sliding off the edge of the bunk. I looked down – I could easily jump the distance to the floor.

A warm hand closed around my ankle. "You have bee…be-yooful legs, Miss M'ria," Charlie slurred, stroking my foot with one hand as he took a deep draught from the bottle with the other.

I laughed, tugging my foot from his grasp as I seized the rum. I tipped the bottle up and drank until someone ripped it from my hands.

"That's enough for you, lass. Hard liquor's not something you should drink too much of." Angrily, I reached for the bottle William held, but he turned away, swallowing the rest. He held the bottle upside down. Not a drop fell from it – he'd emptied it.

I heard a groan and peered down. Charlie was crawling toward the door. He fell face-first into the tin bucket an instant before he vomited explosively and the bucket caught it.

William grasped my still-reaching hand as he set the empty bottle on the locker. "That's what happens when you drink too much. The only cure for it is time." He strode over to Charlie and hauled the boy to his feet. Thrusting the bucket into the boy's hands, he said, "Time to go back to your own cabin to sleep it off, lad. Thank you for sharing your winnings. You'll wish you hadn't won them in the morning, but you'll have to learn some time." He half carried, half dragged the boy into the passage and closed the door. I heard Charlie throw up again before his shuffling steps faded down the corridor.

The liquor in my stomach seemed to ignite, making me see stars. I wanted to kiss William again before the stars faded and maybe more, besides. I swung my legs over the edge of the bunk and jumped. I landed on my feet, but there was something wrong with my head and I seemed to have lost most of the coordination in the rest of my body. I staggered and William caught me. "Easy, lass. You're drunk. I hope you can hold your liquor better than Charlie, for he took the bucket."

I pressed my hands to his cheeks and sucked in a deep breath, my vision blurring as I tried to focus on his lips. Clumsily, I managed to touch my lips to his and memory took control. Or perhaps it was passion. For a moment, he resisted, but the rum seemed to have burned away all resistance and some of the communication barriers between us, too.

Feeling like it was on fire, my body melted in his arms, moulding around his so that we fit together perfectly. Our tongues danced in the fighting ring formed by our lips, but this was different. A desire to feel him on his back beneath me crept into my thoughts and I pushed him toward the bunks, struggling to remember Kaito's moves. Shoulder, waist…yes! William landed on his bunk and I sat astride him, still kissing him with every ounce of my being.

William. I wanted William. I wanted to be as close to him as I could be. To feel his skin against mine as our passion drove us to greater heights. To love him as I'd loved Giuseppe.

Giuseppe.

I drew a sobbing breath as tears cascaded down my cheeks.

William sat up, manoeuvring my body so I sat across his lap, my legs dangling side by side over the edge of the mattress. Firm arms cradled me to his chest as I cried. "It's all right, lass. It was only a stupid wager – I'd never have let anyone hurt you and your honour is safe with me. Even drunk, I could never take advantage of you. You're worth more than that. One day, you'll make the next man you choose to marry very happy. Here, you just hold on to me until you feel better."

I cuddled up to him, revelling in the bliss his arms held, and wondered how I could ever want anyone else but William.

# Thirteen

I squinted up at the ceiling, unable to remember how it had acquired stripes.

Sitting up, I scanned my surroundings. The cabin looked the same, but I was lying in William's bunk and not my own. I'd slept in my rumpled clothes. Ugh. I swore never to do it again — not while I was capable of undressing myself to sleep without them.

William. Where was William?

The door swung silently inwards and I moved into a crouch, ready to spring if my visitor proved a threat.

"Good morning, lass. I brought you some water to wash with – I figured you'd want more privacy than the sailors' washroom. How are you feeling this morning?" William offered his hand and I accepted his help to stand up.

I yelped and wished I hadn't – it felt like another fight had started inside my head and the combatants were trying to beat their way out through my forehead. I pressed my hands to my head and was shocked to discover that it wasn't bulging in the slightest. I whimpered at the pain, just wanting it to stop.

"After that much rum last night, I'm not surprised your head hurts. It does, right?"

I nodded and winced as that made the pain worse. "Hurts," I whispered.

William crouched on the floor beside the bed. "Then you're lucky I know where they keep the medical kit on this boat. The aspirin's gone, but I found something called Aspro that looks like it does the same thing. Here, have you taken pills before?"

I stared at the small, round tablets in his hand, then lifted my eyes to his face. I had no idea what he expected me to do with them.

He smiled. "Good thing I brought a few spare. Right, you put them on your tongue like this." He placed a tablet on his extended tongue, then pulled his tongue back into his mouth. "Take a drink and swallow it down, but don't bite it." He took a mouthful of water and swallowed, then stuck out his bare tongue. "See? Gone. Two should see to your hangover." He pressed two of the tablets into my hand, holding out the cup of water. "Go on."

I stuck my tongue out and laid the pills on it. The taste was unpleasant and they were as dry as bone. I drank some of the water, which filled my mouth with the nauseating taste that remained even after I'd swallowed the tablets. I finished off the cup and hoped the whole ordeal would be worth it. Anything to rid myself of the pounding inside my head.

William pointed at his pillow. "Rest. They

take a little while to work."

I reclined slowly, relieved when the pain lessened as my head hit the pillow. I turned to watch William, hoping he might be able to distract me from my hurting head. He'd removed his shirt and I could see the pale lines of scars on the smooth skin of his back. They looked too straight to be from Portuguese man-o'-war tentacles, as mine were. Perhaps he had different jellyfish in the waters near his home.

He wrapped his fingers around a brush, rotating it into the palm of his other hand until the bristles were covered in creamy foam. To my fascination, he smoothed this foam across his cheeks and his chin. He even spread a thin layer on his upper lip before frothing up a handful more of the stuff to coat his throat. Once he'd carefully rinsed and dried his hands, he unfolded a blade and began sharpening it. The silvery metal glinted in the morning sunlight streaming through the porthole as I wondered why he needed such a sharp edge.

Perhaps I should have felt a premonition of danger, but the blade in William's hands held no fear for me.

"This was my grandfather's," he said, rubbing his thumb across the cream-coloured handle. "Back home, I had one of those modern safety razors, but I had no idea if we could get the blades out here, so I was allowed to take my grandfather's old cut-throat razor. My father never used it – he said a beard was a man's defence against the freezing north wind. My mother said it was a defence against women – if no other woman could find his mouth to kiss, then he was hers forever."

I watched in alarm as he scraped the blade down his own cheek, much like I might have scaled a fish. His careful stroke removed the foam, but his skin beneath it appeared intact. Successive strokes cleared his skin of most of the creamy lather, until he reached his chin. "Did you never watch your father shave? Or your husband?"

I stared, mute, as he continued.

He squinted at a small circle of glass he'd propped up on the locker, puckered his face and cautiously ran the edge of the blade down his chin. He pulled comical faces, pulling the skin this way and that as he scraped the soap away, pausing every few strokes to rinse the blade. When there were only faint lines of foam left and a blob that had somehow adhered to his ear, he splashed water on his face and towelled himself dry.

He lifted the bowl of water, its surface now swimming with the scum of what had once been the lather on his face, and tipped it out the porthole before he turned to face me. I gasped at the transformation.

Gone was the stubble at his throat, the neatly trimmed beard on his chin and the bristly moustache that had adorned his upper lip. His face looked as smooth as mine and I wanted to touch him. I wanted to know what it felt like to kiss him without the tangle of facial hair he'd worn since the day we'd met.

As William buttoned up his shirt, he said,

"When we reach shore, I'll help you find your family so you can go home, where you'll be safe."

I shook my head. "No family. No home. No…more."

William dropped to his knees beside me. "No family left at all? No home? Maria…"

I looked into his horrified eyes and nodded slowly.

Without warning, he gathered me in his arms, pulling me up so that I faced him. Only a breath separated our lips and his eyes drew me deep inside. "I will find a home for you. I swear it. I'll even build one for you with my own hands, if that's what it takes to keep you safe. I'll make a home for you…with you…if that's what you want."

I yielded to the yearning in his eyes, as they reflected the urge in my own heart. I took his head in my hands and kissed him, his tongue gliding around mine as if he wished to hold me inside as well as out.

The door clanged open and we sprang apart.

Charlie stood in the doorway, glowering as he held the frame for support. His hair and his shirt were drenched as if someone had poured a whole bucket of water over them. "I hate rum. I'm never drinking alcohol again." His bloodshot eyes turned pleadingly to me. "Tell me Miss Maria didn't see me in that state."

William eyed him. "Sorry, lad, but she saw everything. I had to turn you out for your own good – and her safety."

Charlie groaned and staggered up the passage, swearing until he was well out of sight and all I could hear of him were his mumbled curses.

"Tidy yourself up, lass, so I can take you to breakfast. I have a surprise for you." William poured clean water into the bowl and offered it to me. I inclined my head in thanks and rolled up my sleeves so I could wash. The whole ocean couldn't wash away the feeling of his mouth on mine and I didn't want it to.

# Fourteen

William's cheeky grin persisted as he led me to the mess deck, which was the scene of unusual activity. Men unrolled lengths of the paper that I'd seen wired to the toilet wall, and painted it red before fastening it to the bulkheads. The stuff hung in swags from the pin points, along the wall and across the ceiling as one man started pinning it to the ceiling beams.

"Interesting decorations," William said, laughing.

One man sniffed and wiped his nose with

the back of his hand, leaving a streak of red paint across his cheek. "Yeah, well we wouldn't have any if it weren't for the Indian boys. No one can find the ones we used for Captain Foster's birthday, so Chief Officer Smith gets ruddy bog-roll instead." He turned to the other men. "Oi, Ali!" Three men responded to his call. "Mr McGregor likes your idea." All three grinned, waved and returned to their work.

William and I carefully made our way through the hall, avoiding the draped, dripping toilet paper. None of the breakfast foods looked particularly appetising and the tea was extra murky this morning, but I tried to choke it down anyway as William seemed set on explaining the occasion to me.

"It's the chief officer's birthday, so we'll be having cake for pudding tonight and the captain has promised he'll get the gramophone out. Smith has an impressive record collection and he picked up some jazz ones in New York that he seemed pretty excited about. He's a big fan of Cole Porter, so I'm sure you'll hear heaps of him tonight. And…speaking of music…" He coughed, looking uncomfortable. "I was wondering if you might be willing…if you'd agree to…if you'd like to…do you know how to dance, Maria?"

"Dance?" I tasted the word, knowing its meaning. I'd lost count of the number of times I'd watched the islanders back home dance at some celebration or other, wishing I could join in, but knowing I could never. The intricate patterns as people spun around each other in matching movements. I'd practiced the steps alone in the dark as the faint strains of the music carried to me across the waves and sand.

"Would you…would you dance with me?" he asked, his voice failing so that he had to clear his throat. "Please?"

Nervously, I wiped my mouth. A small school of frightened fish seemed to have swum into my stomach, it felt so fluttery. For the first time, not to dance alone, in the dark? "Yes, William," I breathed, unable to contain my beaming smile.

"Right now?" he continued, reaching for my hand. Confused, I let him lead me away from the table and out into the watery sunlight at the bow. Didn't we need music? The only sounds were the thrumming of the engines and the sibilance of the waves as they splashed and slid along the hull. He backed away from me a little, placed his hands on his hips, and bowed from the waist. Hurriedly, I did the same.

William grinned at me and raised his hands above his head, clapping to a beat only he could hear. Yet my memory stirred as if I could still hear the faint fiddle floating on the wind. I counted eight before I stretched my toes out to take the first sliding step of a reel I'd only ever danced alone. I lifted my arms above my head, desperately hoping I'd remember the steps as I finished a circuit around William and back to where I'd started. His feet hadn't moved, but he looked astonished. I stopped, looking down at my feet. I'd surely committed some societal faux pas that I didn't understand.

"Maria, where did you learn to dance a reel? Please, let me dance with you," he said eagerly, angling his body like the couples had at home. I matched him, mirroring his motion with each step, tap and turn. I measured my steps carefully, knowing how precise they had to be. Though I should have expected it, when William linked his arm with mine and whirled me around, he left me momentarily breathless. I recovered quickly and remembered the rest of the steps until he touched me again. I laughed aloud for the joy of it – the first time I'd danced with someone else.

The reel ended and he stopped clapping as we both bowed. Still bent over, I gasped when William grasped my shoulders to haul me upright, before he planted a smacking kiss on my lips. "You're better than my sister, Sarah! Where did you learn to dance like that?"

I swallowed, wanting to him to kiss me again instead of asking questions I didn't want to answer. "Home," I responded sadly.

William curled an arm around my shoulder

and stared at the ocean over the starboard railing. "One day, I'd like to take you to my home. You can meet Sarah and her husband, my brothers and their wives, too. I'd wrap you in thick McGregor tartan so you wouldn't feel the cold. Maria, if you let me, I'd take care of you, all your days, in any home you wish." The look in his eyes was one of longing. One I felt I understood – better than his words, at least.

Cautiously, I placed my hands on his cheeks and lifted my lips to his. The kiss we shared was gentle and it seemed to calm his restlessness. He held tight to me as we stared out over the ocean together. My feet tingled to dance some more, but for now I was content in his arms.

# Fifteen

"I'll be right back, lass. Just going to the washroom to make myself look good enough to be seen with you tonight." William winked and closed the door behind him.

Alone in the cabin, I dropped my borrowed pants. The islander girls wore skirts when they danced and I intended to do the same. I stripped the sheet from my bed and checked its width against my legs. Too long, I decided, folding it in half before wrapping it around my waist. I tucked in the top corner, much as the sarong-clad islander girls did, and twisted around, trying to see if it hung straight at the back. I glimpsed someone standing behind me and lifted my eyes to meet William's.

He closed his mouth and shut the door behind him. "You look beautiful," he said. William crossed the cabin so that he was close enough to kiss, but he stood back. "Can I suggest one thing? You should…you should untie your hair. I'm sure one night won't summon disaster. Please?" He caressed my neck, then pulled my braid until the ribbon on the end lay in his fingers. He pulled it off, weaving his fingers through the strands to loosen the braid.

I held my breath, wanting him to continue. Last time he'd used the comb, though, and that was still in my pants pocket. I moved away from him to retrieve it, then held the tortoiseshell comb out to him. "Pl…please?" I asked carefully.

"How can I refuse, when you ask so politely?" His arms circled me, pulling me over to his bunk. We sat so close I could feel the heat of his body behind me. Closing my eyes, I concentrated on his rhythmic strokes as he tamed my hair once more.

"You'll love it. I remember taking Sarah to Hogmanay in Glasgow for the first time. We were dancing what felt like the hundredth reel that night and a storm blew in. A gust of wind caught a fair few kilts up and Sarah screamed. It took me a while to get her to calm down enough to tell me what'd happened. Turns out the breeze had whipped some kilts so high she'd gotten her first glimpse of what a true Scotsman keeps underneath. She wouldn't speak to Angus at all that night – I think she was shocked. James had on a pair of tatty underpants and those caused more trouble than Angus' wedding tackle on display. I think that's the night she first kissed James, too. Ha, all the men made fun of him for wearing anything under his kilt, but Sarah thought he was the most civilised of all of us. It wasn't more'n a year later that she married him, true

Scotsman or no." William chuckled and I felt his breath on my neck a moment before his lips touched my skin. "I'd ask you to be mine, right here and now, if I knew you understood what I was asking, Maria. What've you done to me? I've barely known you a week, but it feels like longer. You've bewitched me so I want no one else – and no future without you in it."

He fell silent and I turned to see the reason for it. His eyes filled with desire and I was no more immune to it than he was. I reached for him even as he reached for me, tangling together in a passionate kiss that stole my breath away. Yet, panting, I puckered up for more. I couldn't seem to get enough of this man and I wanted more.

"We must…must stop," he panted, holding my face in his hands as he pulled away. He seemed to find resistance as difficult as I did. "You look like an angel, Maria, all dressed in white with your gold halo of hair. I'd never forgive myself if I were responsible for the fall of such perfection. I swear, the day you become my wife there'll be no stopping us, but I can't have you until then." He smoothed my shirt down my sides, then paused to fix one of the shell buttons. "Perfect. Shall we go?" He rose and held out his hand. Together, we walked to the mess deck and my first proper party.

# Sixteen

"Maria, you're a very graceful dancer," Captain Foster said as we circled for what felt like the hundredth time this evening. I merely smiled at his evident admiration. It was hard enough to remember the steps of something I'd never danced with others before, let alone with seven men who made mistakes, too.

I crossed the floor again to switch partners and was relieved to find I faced William. The musician fiddling let his last note die away and we bowed. All the men looked flushed and in need of a drink — and I was definitely feeling thirsty, too.

William led me over to a table where one of the stewards was pouring drinks and handed me a partially filled cup. The contents appeared to be a very light coloured tea, but a sniff told me it was as potent as the rum that had tried to make my head explode last night. I tried to hand it back, but William would have none of it. "A girl who can dance a Scottish reel as well as you deserves her dram of good Scottish whisky as much as any man here." The other men we'd danced with, who all held similar cups, laughed. He raised his cup and they followed suit. "To your health on your birthday, Smith!"

Six of them drank. The only man who stood as awkwardly as I did was the first officer — the man whose birthday it was. His eyes met mine and his drink shot into the air. "To the girl who dances like an angel!" All eyes turned to me and a blush crept across my cheeks.

To cover my embarrassment, I took a deep

draught of my drink. And choked on what tasted like liquid coal-smoke.

"Are you all right, lass?" William asked, patting me on the back as I coughed. I managed to shake my head as I doubled over, trying to breathe through my seared throat. "Let's get you outside for some air."

He guided me to the main deck, where the strong wind tried to push us back into the passage. There was so much spray in the air that I tasted salt on my lips. I managed to drag in a lungful of air, then another. I counted five before I straightened again. The whole time, William's hand didn't leave my back — a warm, comforting pressure which reminded me that he cared for me. Even if, once again, he had tried to burn my insides with a drink no sane person should consume.

I heard a faint scratching sound, followed by very different music to the reel melodies we'd danced to. This had a loose feel to it, making it more relaxed. I closed my eyes, feeling the new rhythm.

"Better?" William whispered. His breath tickled my cheek as I nodded. "I missed my steps so many times tonight, for I couldn't take my eyes off you. Every time you were on another man's arm, I wanted to tear you away from him so you'd be mine alone. I want to take hold of you and never, ever let go, Maria. What have you done to me? I was lost at sea until I met you. Now I've found you, I'll cling to you like a barnacle to the hull. I won't be satisfied until you're all mine, lass, even if I have to learn whatever crazy colonial language you speak to make you understand. Please tell me I'm not imagining things and you feel the same. That your heart burns for me as much as mine loves you."

"Love," I rasped hoarsely. I knew the word and its meaning, or I thought I did. Love for someone tucked them safely in your heart for as long as they lived, then ripped your heart asunder when you lost them. I coughed and cleared my throat, trying to find my voice again in my whisky-burned insides.

"I'm so sorry, lass. I should get you another drink."

"Water," I whispered. "No whisky."

William laughed and I followed him back to the mess hall, hoping for a cup of soothing water. He made me sit on one of the benches, which had been pushed back along the wall to make room for the dancing, while he fetched me a cup of something from the steward. I sniffed the liquid experimentally but decided it was probably just water, so I downed it in three gulps. William hovered around me, his every muscle betraying an unusual urgency.

"Love," I began again.

William grasped my hands and moved to sit on the bench beside me. "Love," he said eagerly. "Tell me if you think there's any chance you can love me. I know you barely know me and I'm on my way to a job at the ends of the Earth, or so it feels like, but I have the means to take care of you. And I will."

I managed to smile, but he'd only made it

harder for me to answer him. I barely knew the words to make myself understood as it was.

"Miss Maria! You have to come and dance to this one!" Charlie appeared in front of me, doubled over and panting. "If you dance the Charleston half as well as that strange Scottish fling thing, every man will envy me. Please dance with me."

William's grip on my hands tightened and his voice came out through gritted teeth. "Maria and I are having a private conversation. Go find someone else to dance with, lad."

"You can't keep her all to yourself, Mr McGregor," Charlie persisted. "She's the only woman here and she's not your wife. Maria has the right to dance with whoever she wants to, without your permission. Maria, will you please dance with me?" He held out his hand to me, his eyebrows pulled so low that they seemed to meet over the bridge of his nose.

"Lad, for the last time, leave us alone or…"

"McGregor. A word, please?" Captain

Foster appeared, looking serious.

William looked desperately at me. "Look, captain, I promised I'd take care of Maria tonight. We were —"

"Charlie will take good care of her while you and I have a chat. I'm sure she'd only be bored, listening to talk about the mechanics of the ship. Go on, lad. Maria here is so light on her feet, you'll swear you're dancing with an angel. Don't step on her toes, mind." The captain pried my hands from William's and gestured at the open space where we'd danced earlier. "What girl doesn't love a chance to dance, right, Maria?"

Charlie grabbed my wrist and towed me away from William before I could protest. "He sounds like he's your dad or something. Trying to keep you away from me because I'm not good enough for you. I'm only an apprentice now, but I'll be fully qualified one day, with apprentices of my own. It's not like I'm asking for your hand in marriage. Not yet, anyway. Just a dance. Please, Maria." His eyes mirrored

William's desperation.

I glanced around, but both William and Captain Foster had disappeared. I took a deep breath and summoned a smile for the sweet boy. "Yes, dance."

He seemed incredibly nervous as he stopped and faced me. I felt his arm inch across my back as his clammy hand fastened tightly over my fingers. He counted us in and promptly entered some sort of jerky fit, a grotesque parody of the reel I'd danced earlier with William. I glanced around, but no one seemed to find this unusual.

Charlie grinned. "It's the Charleston. You got to shake your arms and legs about, like this." He demonstrated, letting his arms and legs fly everywhere. A painful kick to my knee made me cry out and his flailing movements ceased as he buried me in a waterfall of apologies.

Seeing my way out of this confusing situation, I hobbled back to the bench with

Charlie trailing behind me. After several seconds, I indicated that I would like a drink and he dashed to the now unmanned drinks table to procure two cups. He presented these to me with unnecessary ceremony, but I smiled and thanked him, all the same. A surreptitious sniff told me it wasn't water, so I carefully set it on the bench beside me. I'd had enough alcohol for one night, if not the next year.

Charlie tossed his back and I realised from his flushed cheeks that this wasn't his first drink of the evening. I fervently hoped he wouldn't be sick again. Perhaps he saw the pity in my eyes, or maybe he'd simply been summoning the courage to act, but the next moment his lips were crushed against mine and his tongue prodded my lips as if he thought I'd grant it entrance. I turned my head away and felt the damp muscle slide along my cheek to my ear. "What's wrong, Maria?" he said thickly. "Haven't you ever been kissed before? You're my first, too."

I leaned back and turned the full force of

my pity on the poor boy. I needed to get these words out right so he'd understand. "I…love William." It came out as barely more than a whisper, but he reacted as if I'd shouted.

Rearing back, he stumbled away from me, hurt. "Maria," he whispered, then bolted out the door to the darkness.

# Seventeen

Alone in a room full of people, I drew my knees up to the bench beside me and closed my eyes, listening to the music from the gramophone. I longed for William to return and hold me again, so I could tell him that he had a place in my otherwise empty heart. Sleepily, I sang along with the melody, so faint I could barely hear my own voice as I thought of William. Not knowing the song's words, I sang my own – calling him to return and claim me.

"Maria."

The unfamiliar voice made me jerk my eyes open. A forest of hands extended toward me as the assembled crew all asked the same thing – requesting that I dance with them.

No. This wasn't possible. They couldn't have heard me – how could they have known what I wanted, from the one man who wasn't among them? I jumped to my feet and shrugged off their pleas. William – where was William? I couldn't see past them to find him.

"No. NO!" I insisted, trying to push through them. I could see the door, but there were too many men in my way. I stumbled on anyway, shoving through them and stepping on my sarong skirt. My knee got caught in the fabric and I fell heavily to the deck. The men seemed to hesitate, before a clamour of voices rose again, offering to help me up. Every man's hands seemed to want to assist, like a million tentacles curling around my body. Between them, they lifted me to my feet, but the sarong had somehow come untied, so it slid to the deck and almost tripped me again as I struggled to escape their kind but misguided attention. I fought my way free from its folds and hurried to the exit. I wanted to scream at them to leave me alone and not touch me, but I didn't know the words.

I almost made it before a dark shadow barred my way. Two more hands grasped my shoulders and my tears of fury spilled over. "NO!" I cried, trying to push the man out of my way.

"What's wrong, Maria?" William asked gently, taking in my messy appearance. When his gaze reached my bare, bruised knees, his expression tightened. "What happened? Where is your skirt?"

Now the tears had started, I couldn't seem to turn them off. Faster they fell as I tried to pull out of his grasp so I could go hide in my cabin. I'd had enough revelry and dancing for one night – for all my nights.

"It's all right, lass," he said. I cried out in alarm as he swept me up in his arms. My feet grazed the bulkhead — the passage wasn't wide enough for this.

"McGregor," the captain began. I hadn't seen him standing in the shadows beside William. Had he witnessed my weakness, too? I struggled to be set on my own feet again.

Looking hurt, William gave me my freedom. "I swore I'd keep her safe and I won't break my promise. It's your ship and they're your crew — you sort them out. All I'm worried about is Maria."

Captain Foster sighed. "Take care of her, then, and find her some clothes. God only knows what happened this time and she surely won't tell us. Go on." He waved his hands in the direction of the sleep cabins.

Cautiously, I took William's hand. I took two steps toward our cabin, but he hadn't moved, letting my arm stretch out behind me. One more step and I'd have to let go. I didn't want to. "No hurt," I said slowly. "No more dance." I laid my cheek on the back of my hand, as I'd seen him do when he slept, and closed my eyes. "Rest."

Perhaps in the morning I'd have the courage to tell him the secrets of my heart.

# Eighteen

I turned over in my narrow bunk, hoping to find some spot that was more comfortable, but it was no use. It wasn't the music I could still hear from the party in progress keeping me up, either. No matter how I lay, I still felt the grasping hands on my body, wanting more from me than I was willing to give. How had a ship full of sane men suddenly become one crewed by lust-crazed monsters? I wanted the comfort of William's arms around me to drive away the sensation of his shipmates' assault.

Peering down at the bunk below me, I wondered if I could persuade him. His soft snores told me I'd have to wake him first, or slip into his arms as he slept and hope that would be enough.

The more I resisted the urge, the more I ached for him until I finally gave in and climbed down the ladder to the floor. I slipped beneath the blanket, cuddling up to his warm body, to find the man slept in a vest and some sort of short pants, instead of naked as I did. After a few minutes, his arms closed around me, just like I wanted, as he seemed to rouse. "Maria?" he murmured.

"Yes, William," I whispered back, pressing my body close against his. I could feel his arousal and I suddenly wanted that, too. A hot, passionate encounter to drive the day out of my mind. I slipped my hands into his shorts, stroking his hard length. I wanted him so badly – I'd never felt such longing for Giuseppe.

Forgive me, Giuseppe, but William is warm and here and you can never hold me in your arms again as you tell me you love me, I thought. And William, William…

William woke and I had no thoughts left for Giuseppe – only for the man beside me, who had ripped his clothing off. He stroked my breasts and belly so hard it seemed as if he wanted to leave bruises beneath his fingers. His hands dipped lower still, setting my thighs on fire as he caressed those, too, parting my legs. His fingers slipped inside me at the top of each stroke, trailing wetness down my inner thighs before stroking inside for more.

I moaned without words for the pleasure he gave me and how much more I craved. He seemed to understand exactly what I wanted. William's hands wrapped around my thighs, his fingers spreading my lower lips wide. He lifted me as he shifted so that I was poised above his hard head, wet and waiting. I tried to squirm down onto him, but all I managed to do was drive his fingers deeper. "Oh, yes," I moaned, wanting more. He slammed me down against him, as he drove up inside me.

"Oh God, Maria," he groaned, drowning out whatever sounds I made. Blissfully, I tried to hold tight to his hard heat inside of me, but he withdrew almost completely before he thrust deeply again. The harder I tried to hold onto him, the more molten my insides seemed to become until a volcanic burst of pleasure made me sob his name. I felt him chuckling, though he still filled me, as he said, "Oh, I can do better than that, lass. Hold tight." He seized my hips and ground me against him with each slow thrust, the steady rhythm building the heat hotter still.

"Oh, yes, yes, William…oh…OH!" When this stunning rush hit, he fastened his mouth on my bouncing breast, sucking so hard I thought he'd take the nipple off. He licked and kissed his way across my chest to the other nipple, suckling gently while I clenched him tightly between my legs. Still shaking, I wanted more of the pleasure this man could give me and I started riding him, like a boat rides a wave. Flying over the crest, then slamming down into the trough, spreading my legs wider to drive him as deep inside me as he could go, my hips rocking as the heat built inside me so slowly I thought I'd scream before it released.

His mouth still wrapped around my breast, William grasped my hip with one hand, grinding me against him again as his other hand slipped between us. I was already full of him – what else did he think he could fit inside me? He pinched something between my lower lips, rubbing the swollen flesh hard between his fingers and I let out a wordless sob as the sensation overwhelmed me. I barely felt the sting of his teeth on my nipple as I screamed his name until I was hoarse.

William kissed me into silence as he flipped our bodies over so that he was on top and my head rested on his pillow. He plunged deep inside me again and I grasped his behind with shaking hands, wanting to push him deeper still. I spread my legs wider, lifting them to give him better access to all of me. He chuckled again and pulled my legs over his shoulders, thrusting so hard and deep I felt him hit a fleshy wall inside me. And again. And again…he pounded me endlessly, not stopping even when I breathlessly cried out his name as yet another rush of pleasure rocked me. Nor did I want him to stop. Ever. Feeling as if I'd explode if I came again, I was helpless to resist as William carried me to the crest before he slowed his pace as if he were teasing me. I clenched every muscle in my midsection, trying to hold on to him as he almost pulled out before plunging inside me again.

"You're close, aren't you, sweetheart? So am I. But ladies must come first. I insist…"

I moaned, arching my back up. His mouth covered mine, taking my voice, my tongue and muffling the scream that threatened to escape when he drove me to peak again. I was so close and I wasn't sure how my body would bear it. None of my time with Giuseppe had prepared me for this.

His fingers slipped between my lower lips again, pinching harder than ever, but he swallowed the sound of my squeal as he teased me closer and closer to the edge. A tortuously slow thrust made me gasp as his fingers circled, rubbing skin so sensitive it felt like my nerves were raw and he played them like the strings of the fiddle we'd danced to only hours before. When I thought only the tiniest movement would be enough to seal my fate, William pulled out of me entirely. I didn't have time to protest before he slammed back in, so hard, rough and fast that I was catapulted into my final, cataclysmic orgasm without warning. A scream ripped out of my throat, but his mouth on mine muffled the sound as I felt him burst inside me, a hot spurt that filled me completely.

He toppled over onto his side, his head hitting the pillow beside me. I tightened my limbs around him, wanting to savour the feeling of him inside me until he inevitably softened and slipped out. But for now, we were one, as we snuggled together into satisfied sleep.

162

# Nineteen

Morning dawned and William's body was warm beside mine, though I felt empty without him inside me. The hard, hot length pressed against my thigh told me that he was ready for more action and the very thought of him had me aching in anticipation. I tipped us so that he lay on his back and I sat astride him, gasping as I guided him inside me. In the morning light, I saw how big the man was and spread my legs wider to take his whole length. No wonder I ached so much — but it was a sweet ache, that could only be soothed with more, equally hot sex. I slipped up and down his shaft, working my hips so that he slid against that sweet spot inside me with every stroke. He started to lift his hips to meet mine, driving him deeper inside me, and I squeezed him as he reached the peak of each thrust.

"Mmmm," William said as his hands closed around my breasts, which bounced as my body moved.

Like last night, I felt the slow build before my bubble burst, though it was nowhere near as powerful as the pleasure William could wring from my body when I was no longer in control. I longed to wake him properly so that we could do it all again. Perhaps I could rouse him with a little pleasure of my own…

I rode him harder, clenching my inner muscles in rhythm with the movement.

"Oh God, Maria," he groaned as I felt the triumph of his hot release inside me. For a moment, his dreamy smile matched my own as

I looked down at him over my breasts. If only it could have lasted.

A loud crash sounded from somewhere above and we both jerked in shock. William's expression changed from bemused bliss to panic as he took in our intimately intertwined bodies. "Oh my God, Maria, we didn't. I thought it was a dream and then I woke up and you…oh God." He pushed me off him and stood, striding over to the water jug to splash some on his face and his nether regions. Keeping his back to me, he pulled on some clothes, muttering under his breath so that I couldn't discern the words.

I stood, too, dropped so quickly from bliss to rejection. A trickle of fluid tracked down my thigh, but I ignored it. I didn't understand. Last night, he'd enjoyed every moment and this morning, too, I'd thought until he'd pushed me away.

"Where in hell are your clothes? For God's sake, get dressed." He barely glanced at me before he left the cabin, slamming the door shut behind him.

Tears flowed down my cheeks as I climbed the ladder to retrieve my shirt and my pants. Following William's cold example, I splashed some water between my legs to cool the hot flesh where I'd held him so tightly, only minutes before, then poured a little down the breasts he'd tenderly cupped in his hands. I pulled my pants on and slipped the shirt over my head, not caring that my passion-hardened nipples were clearly outlined through the damp fabric. I tucked my comb into my pocket, wanting to ask William if he could comb my hair and braid it again for me, for it was still undone from last night. But first, I needed to find him.

Swiping the tears from my face, I strode out into the passage, intent on making him tell me what I'd done wrong. I had no idea how I'd manage to ask him, nor whether I'd understand his explanation, but I had to try. I didn't want to make the same mistake again – I wanted to share more nights like last night with him. Forget Giuseppe, for he was cold and dead – he could never touch me and heat my blood again. I wanted William, forever and always.

Someone grabbed my arm and something hard struck my face. I found myself lying on the deck, staring up at the blank bulkhead before a boot came into view. It kicked me in the head and everything faded to black.

# Twenty

I awoke to darkness and the creaking of metal under strain. I woke to aching and pain, too, as I tenderly touched my bruised face, remembering the blows that had knocked me unconscious. How much time had passed?

In the lack of light, it was impossible to judge time, so I didn't. More important was where I'd been lying – somewhere below decks and below the waterline, too, if the bulkheads made so much noise. I shouted, listening to the echo of my voice to judge the size of my prison. The echo was decidedly hollow – placing me in one of the large cargo holds.

First, I had to find my way out. There were three possible exits – the hatch in the ceiling or the hatch in the wall that led to the lower deck, both of which were kept firmly closed most of the time, or through the hull – but that would sink the ship. The ceiling hatch was too high for me to reach – unless I stood on the shadowy cargo. Standing on the edge of the catwalk that ran along the side of the hold, I stretched my foot out toward the flat substance filling the hold almost to the level of the catwalk. My toes sank into what felt like wet beach sand until most of my foot was covered with the stuff. I wasn't sure how deep the hold went, but I didn't trust the mud that filled it to hold my weight. That ruled out the ceiling hatch.

With considerable difficulty, I pulled my foot free of the sucking mud and headed along the catwalk toward the door hatch. This one I could reach easily – it was a door, after all –

but there was no way to open it. A piece of metal in the middle told me that there had once been a valve wheel attached to the door for precisely this purpose, but my jailer had removed it before imprisoning me here.

I hammered on the door, shouting until my sore throat stole my capacity for sound. Last night I'd screamed for joy as William made my body sing in ways I couldn't have imagined and today I paid the price — I didn't have a strong enough voice to scream for help. I pounded on the door for a few more seconds, but I received no response. That left only one means of escape — the one that could kill everyone else on board.

Padding along the catwalk in my bare feet, I scanned the bulkhead that I knew was the inner wall of the hull, searching for its weak points. I'd seen where shells had pierced the *Emden*'s hull, almost a decade ago, but the greatest damage had been where the hull plates met and the joins had come undone in the force of shell impacts. This vessel's plates were riveted together and the round rivets stood out in long rows, like regimented barnacles. There was one place that the rows weren't regular – a metal plate, perhaps half the size of the door, covered a section of bulkhead. Water seeped out from the bottom of the plate, creating a slow trickle into the slushy cargo. If I wanted a weak point, I'd found it – for the vessel had already sprung a slight leak here. All I'd need was something to pry the rivets from the panel and I could swim out of here, right up to the surface.

I searched the hold for some sort of pry bar that I could use and I found the next best thing – two shovels, attached to the catwalk with a length of rope, but the shovels themselves were partially submerged in the ooze. I pulled them out and set to work, untying the water-swollen hemp. It felt like forever before I'd freed them, but I had little else to do.

Setting the edge of the shovel against the lowest rivet, I slowly leaned my weight on the handle. The rusty rivet snapped, increasing the trickle to a rivulet down the side of the ship. I examined the remaining rivets, which looked equally corroded. With my shovel, I'd make short work of this and then what? If I reached the surface, I'd still be climbing aboard a sinking ship in the middle of the ocean. At best, I could save William and some of the crew before she sank, but what if my imprisonment was at the captain's command with the crew's acquiescence? They'd take me prisoner once more on the lifeboat, in much closer quarters than here. Why had they locked me in here, anyway? Was it just one person, or the whole crew who'd locked me up?

I barely knew any of these men. Even William, who'd loved me one minute and rejected me the next. For the first time, I longed to be home. No matter how vicious the old women at home were, they'd never lock me up in the bowels of a ship. Instead, they'd banished me to the freedom of the outside world.

I sank to the floor, uncertainty overwhelming me. I was no longer a child – I knew the consequences of sinking a ship and killing those on board. A shipwreck had brought Giuseppe to my arms, too. William. I couldn't kill William. Not unless I knew for certain that he'd condemned me to this prison.

One thing I swore: the men who had would die.

Hefting the shovel once more, I drove it against the next rivet, which crumbled like old bread.

Clanking across the hold froze me, followed by a man's voice swearing. I gripped my shovel and stepped softly along the catwalk. My jailer had returned and the only one who would leave this hold alive was me.

# Twenty One

The furtive manner of the man who swung the door open told me more than any of his words. He was afraid of being discovered here. He wouldn't be so fearful if his actions were sanctioned by the rest of the crew. I smiled in the darkness. Today, he would die.

"I say it's bad luck to bring a woman aboard. Sciarra says it's the best kind of luck. Whores like you keep the men happy on a long voyage," a nasal voice said, followed by the clang of him pulling the hatch closed behind him. Closed but not locked, for the valve wheel was still missing. He clicked on a handheld light, a tube that directed a beam of light from one end, and pointed it at the catwalk. "I heard you scream for McGregor last night. Only whores make that much noise – normal girls just lie passive, waiting for the fucking to finish. So you can scream for me, too. Down here where no one, not even your precious McGregor, will hear you. If you make me happy, I might decide to keep you instead of throwing you overboard for the sharks."

Sharks I knew. I wished I had a school of them now, to feed his screaming body to.

The light beam swung closer to where I stood on the catwalk with my shovel raised. Three more steps, two, one…I swung my weapon with all my strength, but I'd misjudged the man's height and I hit his shoulder and not his head. He roared and backhanded me so that I crashed to the catwalk, my breath knocked from my lungs. The shovel flew out of my hands and into the ooze.

The man threw his weight on top of me, wrapping his arm around my neck and dragging me up by the throat. "You'll pay for that, whore." His arm tightened around my throat so that I could barely breathe.

My life would not end like this. Not on a raft in the middle of the ocean; not in bed without ever regaining consciousness; and not at the hands of this sterling example of human chivalry. I just had to work out how I intended to kill him. I wanted it to be slow and painful…and I wanted to watch. Sharks…I'd settle for just one of the beasts right now.

The bastard let go of my throat, hefting my body as if to throw me. I braced myself for the blow, for it was sure to hurt, and laughed as my body smacked into the cold mud. I looked up at the hatch above me and stretched out on the surface of the slurry. He'd made a deadly mistake that he wouldn't survive to regret.

A rough hand grasped my leg, dragging me back onto the catwalk, before a hand fastened on my hair. He dragged me along the metal before throwing me against the bulkhead beside the weeping panel.

A booted foot slammed into my ribs. "Ready to lie down and take it, whore?"

"No," I managed to say before he kicked me again. His hands tore at my pants, but the fabric was too thick to rip, so he swore some more. A smile sprang to my lips as I balled up a fist, socking him right in the fork. Oh, it felt satisfying to cause him pain.

"Bitch!" He let go of me for a moment and I drew a deep, burning breath. He lunged for me again with murder in his eyes.

I rolled and grabbed the other shovel, raising it to hit him with it. He deflected the blow, so it clanged against the bulkhead instead. A rivet clattered to the catwalk. We fought for the shovel, both pinning it against the hull, and I felt it grind through one rivet and then another. The panel slid beneath me as water splashed my bare feet. I hadn't wanted to sink the ship, but this bastard had forced my hand. So be it.

I threw myself back into the inky mud, splaying out my limbs so I'd stay on the surface. The metal panel broke free, forced inward by the weight of the Indian Ocean fighting for entry. I watched him flounder on the edge, trying not to fall in with me, and my smile widened. The water flowing in formed a layer on top of the mud, floating my body free. I ducked beneath the surface, swimming to the eddy that swirled behind him.

"You have to surface some time, bitch, you can't swim forever. And when you do, I have a surprise waiting for you." He grasped his crotch with one hand. The surprise looked particularly small, even to my inexperienced eyes.

"Come on out!" he called, looking at the spot where I'd submerged, unaware that I'd surfaced behind him. His eyesight must be worse than I thought. He couldn't see death lurking in the shadows. All the better for my surprise.

I started to sing, keeping my voice so soft it was beyond the range of human hearing, yet I could see it affecting him. His body grew rigid and his eyes widened. I increased the volume so that he could hear me, but the only part of him that moved was his increasingly furious expression.

"Come on in," I said slowly, beckoning as I hoped he understood.

The man staggered toward the water, his fear increasing with every step. I sang again, louder still, and his pace increased. Two more steps. One. He splashed into the water, feet first, and his boots dragged him deep into the mud beneath the surface, where he couldn't breathe. He stood like a statue, desperately trying to move as he held his breath. Ah, but this man was in my world now and he would never leave it.

I dove under the surface, so that I could float face to face with him as he died. I wondered if he could see me as well as I saw him, but I didn't care. This was for my satisfaction and not his.

When death claimed him, his arms lifted from his sides and his head sagged – my control over his body died with him. Leaving the corpse behind, I shot to the surface before I was forced to swim through the filth that his body expelled. Drowned men voided their bowels like any other dead body.

I eyed off the hole in the hull. Water was pouring in so fast that there was nothing I could do to stop the flow. I couldn't save the ship, but perhaps I could save some of its crew if I hurried. Hauling myself out onto the catwalk, I slammed the door open and sprinted down the passage and up the ladder to the crew quarters. Darkness followed me, for it was night time and most of the lights were dimmed for sleep.

I shook the young apprentice awake. "Charlie. Ship is sinking."

The boy grumbled under his breath but didn't wake, so I took a deep breath and started to sing again. If I could control the angry attempted rapist, the sympathetic Charlie would be no problem, I hoped. "Ship sinking. Save…everyone," I told the boy.

The boy nodded and crawled out of bed, heading for the captain's cabin. I hid in the shadows while I watched him hammer on the captain's door and tell him of the impending disaster. Satisfied, I headed up to the deck. The sea surface looked closer than it had since I'd boarded…just a short jump and I'd be swimming again. I glanced back at the men clambering into the lifeboats. For a moment, I considered killing them all so that none would live to tell the tale of the girl they'd found floating in the middle of the ocean. They'd let the bastard imprison me, after all. Even if they hadn't condoned his actions, they hadn't stopped him or tried to help me.

No. Their chances of survival were slim enough without my interference. Sober, most of them were kind men who deserved a chance at life. Aside from the angry man who'd hurt me, of course. The man who would have hurt me much earlier if it hadn't been for William. Wait, William – where was he? I didn't see him on the lifeboats – he must still be below. I couldn't let him drown. I dashed for the hatch.

I'd barely made it down the first two steps before strong arms grabbed me, smashing my body against the bulkhead. Pain exploded as another rib fractured and I heard my voice cry out before a hand clamped over my throat, cutting off my air.

"He said it was bad luck to bring a woman aboard. What'd you do to Barrett?" my assailant demanded. Sciarra – Barrett's friend.

I attempted to swallow, but I couldn't. I couldn't even draw in enough breath to speak. William would die if this man prevented me from waking him. No. I wouldn't let that happen.

He slammed me against the bulkhead again, further abusing my already bruised body. "I found him in the hold. You didn't know he was meeting me there, did you? You killed him and sank the ship, bitch. You're trying to kill us all – just like I bet you did to your last ship. And I'm going to make sure you…gurnghk!"

I dropped my knee from his crushed balls, sucking in a deep breath. "William!" I screamed. I had to save him – there was so little time. The ship was sinking fast.

Sciarra's fist met my jaw, engulfing my head in blinding blackness, and I crumpled to the deck. He was on top of me, wrenching at my pants before I could even see. "I'm going to fuck you right here outside the captain's cabin for that, bitch. And then I'm going to leave you here to drown with the ship."

I gritted my teeth. "No."

My pants ripped and a meaty hand bruised the bare skin of my thigh. His other hand fumbled between us for his own pants as he shoved his knee between my legs. "Yes," he grunted.

"No," another voice said as a gaff slammed

into the side of Sciarra's head. Sciarra crashed against the bulkhead and didn't rise – I hoped he'd been knocked out cold. He and Barrett had agreed to meet in the hold, where they'd imprisoned me. Both of them had planned to rape me and neither would survive the night, I vowed.

A clatter caught my attention as William threw the gaff down and extended his hand. "Are you all right?" he asked as he helped me to my shaky feet.

I nodded, swallowing in the hope of finding my voice. "Thank you, William."

He grinned. "Any time, lass. I'm sorry I didn't come sooner – before he hurt you." He waved at my torn clothes, reddened, and averted his eyes. I glanced down. My breasts were visible through my torn shirt and my pants hung low on my hips, exposing more skin. I tried to cover myself up with the shredded shirt, but I fought a losing battle. "Let me get you another shirt. I'll have to buy more when we make port – I've never met a woman who liked to destroy my clothing so much." He took my arm and tried to pull me into his cabin. "I've been looking for you all day. I need to explain, to apologise, to–"

I shook my head and pulled back. "Ship sinking. Must go." I pointed in the direction of the lifeboats above. It was my turn to tug on his arm, trying to convey my urgency. I didn't know the right words to make him move. "Not…die," I said. I turned away, almost crying with relief when I felt the heat of his body against my back. I scrambled up the ladder, trying to keep my pants from tangling around my ankles. Strong arms encircled my waist, holding my pants in place as he lifted me to the deck. My skin tingled from the touch and I wanted him to touch more, but that could cost him his life. I needed to get him to a lifeboat.

His longer strides carried him ahead of me, so it wasn't long before he was dragging me behind him and I struggled to keep up as my sinking pants threatened to trip me. "Maria!"

he called, glancing back. "Maria, hurry!"

I did hurry, but the ship gave a lurch and I tripped, losing my grip on my pants.

"Don't be afraid, lass. I'll keep you safe." William scooped me up in his arms and carried me to the lifeboat. He passed me to the other crewmen before scrambling in after me. They started lowering the boat into the water and I turned my gaze to the dark surface beneath us. Adrift on the ocean again – perhaps that was my fate. At least the ocean's depths would claim my attackers. Ocean's justice. I smiled.

# Twenty Two

"Sciarra!" a voice shouted. "The ship's sinking, man! Get into the lifeboat before you drown! We'll swing around and pick you up!" I stared at the ship, now sitting far too low in the water. Waves were already washing across the deck — the *Treversa* wouldn't remain on the surface much longer. Yet as I watched, a figure staggered and splashed to the remaining lifeboat. Sciarra. If he reached it, he'd survive.

NO.

I tensed, readying my muscles for flight. I

could remain in the lifeboat with William and the non-hostile crew, perhaps even helping them to safety, or I could ensure the violent bastard died for his crimes. Bitterness and bile or fleeting hope?

Men started shouting about cutting the boat free before the ship dragged us down with her. Panic ensued as several men sawed at the ropes holding us to the sinking ship and I saw my chance.

William grabbed my arm. "No, lass. Stay with me so I can make amends to you for last night. You don't owe the man anything. He'll reach the lifeboat and have as much chance as any of us. Don't risk your life for him."

I melted beneath his cold fingers, wishing I could simply sink into those welcoming arms and forget all that had happened since they had last held me. But I did not forget, nor forgive. The violent human had hurt me and he would pay the highest price the ocean could offer. I sprang, clearing the distance between the lifeboat and the sinking vessel, and grabbed the rail. Laboriously, I hauled my aching body aboard to the sound of William shouting himself hoarse. A wave crashed over me, filling my mouth with seawater as it knocked me flat. I coughed up a lungful of liquid and felt a searing pain in my scalp.

"I knew you wanted me. Now we'll have a boat all to ourselves until we reach land. You're going to learn to please me, bitch, or I'll let you drown like Barrett," Sciarra said as he dragged me across the deck, his hands knotted in my hair. He threw me into a lifeboat and the impact made me expel all my breath in one hit, so I could neither breathe nor respond. It didn't matter – he needed to cut the lifeboat free from the ship before he could hurt me again. This time, I'd be ready. I pulled a breath into my searing lungs, followed by another. Quietly, I began to sing – a different song to the one I'd sung in the hold. This one had teeth and blood lust to boot, for this song had sunk the *Emden*.

The keel bumped across the railings and I

saw the ship loom above us as she tipped on her side, hiding William and the rest of the crew from me – and us from them, I realised. It was now or never. I struggled to stand, surveying the swell. Did I imagine it, or did a fin cut the water of a wave? No, there was another…and another. Sharks and shipwreck – a duo Sciarra would not survive. Not to mention me.

Sciarra sawed through the last of the ropes and sank to the bench seat before he saw me. "Get down, bitch." He brandished a knife. The blade glinted in a flash of lightning.

I shook my head and smiled at him. Moving my weight from one foot to another, I started to rock the boat. He clung to the sides, shouting at me to stop. I shifted faster, letting the gunwales touch the water before moving my weight to the other foot. I raised my voice, singing loud enough for him to hear me over the storm. He slashed at me with the knife, but I dodged and he overbalanced. He landed on top of the blade, skewering his hand. He gave a roar and leaped to his feet, charging at me.

I jumped, landed hard, and felt the boat tip beneath me, throwing us both into the waves. Cold water kissed my skin as I pulled off my ripped pants so that I could shift to my true form. I clothed myself in my own skin – the shallow-water blue of a Maori wrasse – and opened my gills to take a life-giving breath from my ocean home. Behind me, the sound of stressed steel screeched beneath the surface as the ship sank. I breathed deep, letting the draught of dissolved oxygen cool my instincts to those of the killer I knew myself to be. I blew spent water out of my gills, taking another gulp before I searched for my prey.

Heedless of the sharks, Sciarra swam for the boat, trailing blood behind him like burley. I darted toward him, overtaking the human easily, and seized his foot, dragging him down to where he couldn't breathe. His face showed his panic as his arms clawed wildly for the surface.

I raised my voice and sang a command to

the sharks, which started an intricate, spinning dance around their supper. He screamed sweetly as they shredded him, piece by piece until the screaming ceased.

Blood swirled in the turbulent water as the sharks churned it further, looking for more to eat. None were frenzied enough to approach me, but my pants were not so lucky. Two sharks fought over the floating fabric, thrashing the water into foam so that I didn't see the boat approaching until it was above me.

"Maria!" William's anguished cry smote my heart.

Oars scattered the sharks and one carefully lifted my shredded clothing from the water.

"Those were Maria's," I heard William's voice say. "The sharks must have…oh God, I hope she didn't suffer. She saved us all – even tried to save Sciarra. She was an angel sent to save us all."

I itched to surface and show them that I still

lived, but caution stayed my fins. I'd need to shift back into my human form without them seeing my tail and that took time. It would be dangerous for them, too, with hungry sharks still swimming nearby. I was safer beneath the surface and lost to them.

"God rest her soul," said another man. "The ocean takes her own. Always has."

Yes. The elders of this ocean might reject me, but the ocean herself never would. I was one of the people of the ocean's gift, after all, and this was my home.

"Time to set sail. If we mean to survive, we must make Madagascar or Mauritius. Land is to the north-west and a long way from here. The men who take first watch may have the first cigarette ration when the storm is over. Volunteers?"

My mangled pants landed in the water above me and something golden-brown slipped from the pocket. My comb — the gift from William. The only thing I owned and it was sinking. I dove after it, snatching it from the water. This wasn't my home any more – home was with William. I surged to the surface.

The boat was gone. I rose to the crest of a wave, searching the ocean for my love. A glimpse of white in the trough between waves, far from me, told me I was too late. I could never catch up to them now. The boat sported a tall mast and a white sail caught the gale, driving them in the direction of land. I farewelled William with my eyes, not daring to say the words aloud as he sailed away with my heart.

I wondered what to do now. I couldn't return to my people, so my choices were a solitary existence out here or an attempt to reach land and make a life among humans. Men like Sciarra and Barrett – but men like Giuseppe and William, too.

If I hadn't stupidly pursued my trinket, I might have shared the lifeboat with William and I'd be winging my way to a human life with him. Instead, I had the open ocean and an overturned lifeboat all to myself. Wearily, I sent a wave to tip my boat upright as I shifted my tail to legs and hauled myself over the gunwale. I tucked the precious comb into my hair.

The bottom of the boat was awash, so I opened one of the footlockers, searching for a bucket. Instead, I found a sail and some tins of condensed milk. Further scrabbling unearthed a can opener, so I pried the milk can open and drank the lot. The sweetness made me gag, but it seemed wasteful to pour the milk over the side. Using the empty can, I bailed water from my boat until my arms were too tired to lift the tin any more. I wrapped myself in the sail and stretched my aching body along the bottom, letting exhaustion and sleep claim me. At least I had a boat to sit in while I awaited rescue from the next passing ship — far better than the raft I'd borrowed last time.

# Twenty Three

I woke in daylight, squinting at the grey clouds that gave no indication of the time of day. The storm wasn't over yet.

My boat had taken on more water overnight, topped up by my tears at losing William, so I found the floating milk can and returned most of the seawater to the ocean. By the time I was done, my stomach demanded breakfast. I eyed off the milk cans in the locker before closing it firmly. I'd had enough human food for a while. With no humans in sight, I chose a more tempting meal.

I lowered my aching body over the side and into the numbing water. I dipped my face beneath the surface and started to sing, careful to keep one hand firmly on my boat. The fish that answered my call was precisely what I wanted – a small wahoo, young enough to be curious, but big enough to make a meal. One snap of his spine was all it took to end his life before I threw him into the boat. I hoisted myself in after him and proceeded to eat my fill of his dense flesh. The wahoo certainly beat a fresh tuna, not to mention a marmite sandwich. Humans ate some very strange things.

Feeling pleasantly full, I threw his bony carcass into the waves and reclined. For a long time, I watched the clouds until the day turned to dark night with no stars or moon in sight.

Once again, I curled up under the sail and sank into slumber.

# Twenty Four

The boat rocked beneath me, reminding me of the lifeboat I should have been on. The one that the crew had winched into the water. The one I hoped still held the man I wished I was with. William.

Light blinded me and my heart leaped, for the light came not from the sun but from one of the handheld tubes William had called a torch. "William?" I asked.

"Get the captain. He needs to see this," an unfamiliar male voice said. Not William.

"Yes, Mr Alexander." Footsteps on the deck faded away.

Mr Alexander directed the light away from my eyes and my sight slowly returned. "Were you on the *Trevessa*?' he asked.

Pressing my lips tightly together, I nodded. If they'd found my boat, perhaps they'd also found the other lifeboats and rescued the man I loved. Tears sprang to my eyes. "William?"

Another face peered down at me.

"Captain?" Mr Alexander said quietly.

The new man shook his head. "I've never seen the girl before in my life. She's in one of the *Trevessa*'s lifeboats, yet there's no record of a woman aboard the ship. There was a William listed as a passenger. Some Scottish name. McKenzie or something. Is that the man you mean, girl? William McKenzie?"

I swallowed. "William McGregor," I whispered.

"Was he on the lifeboat with you? For you were the only one in it when we found you." I shook my head and he continued, "We haven't found the other lifeboats – only yours."

William wasn't here. I should have followed his boat and kept him safe. I started to sob, covering my face with my arms so the men wouldn't see my naked grief. A light touch traced the bruised flesh of my arm.

"Did McGregor do this to you?"

I shook my head violently, glaring at the captain for even suggesting such a thing.

"Fetch Mrs D'Angelo and ask her to meet us in her cabin. Explain to her that we need her help on a matter of utmost secrecy – and it's an emergency."

Mr Alexander nodded, striding out of my field of vision. The captain remained.

"I'm Captain Dunnet of the *Trevean*. We're searching for survivors from the *Trevessa* and you're the first we've found. We'll keep looking – no sign of the other lifeboats is a good sign. Do you know if they made it to the boats before the ship sank?"

I nodded.

Captain Dunnet pressed, "Was your William

aboard your boat?" I shook my head. "Then there's hope for him yet. If we don't find him, the other boats may reach land. Captain Foster was a good man and a good friend. If McGregor is with Foster, then he has a better chance at sea than any man alive."

He reached for me and I cowered against the boards at the bottom of the lifeboat, pulling the sail close around me. He sighed. "Not all men are like the ones who hurt you. I'm here to help." He held out his hand and I took it, accepting his help to rise to my feet, clutching the sail to hide my nakedness. I wasn't going to make the mistake of showing my body to the men of this ship as I had the last — I'd been through enough. I wanted to take a rest from killing people so that I could learn what it was to be human. To become one of them, if only for a little while.

Holding Captain Dunnet's hand, I followed him down the ladder to my new cabin.

# Twenty Five

Two steps inside, I stopped dead. It appeared I was to share this cabin, too, but with William's opposite.

Instead of a smiling young man, I met the gaze of a frowning older woman. Her cold eyes drifted from me to the captain. I heard the click as he closed the door behind him.

"If you expect me to keep her condition a secret, you're sorely mistaken. No woman deserves to be beaten like this. Where did you find her and who is responsible for the deplorable act?" Her voice rang with authority – she sounded like my mother.

Captain Dunnet's voice was low as he replied, "We fished up one of the *Trevessa*'s lifeboats today and found her aboard. Whoever did this was aboard the *Trevessa*. There are no women listed as passengers, so she must have been a stowaway or someone smuggled her aboard. Even a stowaway's entitled to some dignity – to be put ashore at the next port, in the hands of the authorities, but it looks like she was kept a secret and...ill-used instead. Now, we're committed to searching for survivors, but if the rest of the crew hear of this, half of them will want to call off the search, while the other half will want to continue, to bring the offenders to justice. If we find survivors, what will happen if we bring aboard the men who did this to her? I'm asking you to keep her hidden from the crew and keep her safe until we reach port in Fremantle."

I returned the woman's stare with fish-cold

eyes. The two humans might be engaging in a power struggle, but I wouldn't submit to either of them. I'd killed two men and sunk one ship already this week – what was one more?

"Very well. Someone must take care of the girl, so I shall. But if the men who did this survive the shipwreck, heaven help them, for I will see them charged for this." The woman waved him away and he left without another word.

"Sit down," she said to me, gesturing at the bunk. I perched on the edge of the mattress, tucking the sail around me. She continued to stare at me, her eyes raking me from top to toe. After some time, she sank onto the bunk opposite me. "What's your name?"

"Maria."

"Tell me what happened."

I swallowed. I didn't know the words to explain half of it, but I was determined to try. "Ship sank."

She shook her head and pointed at my arm. "To you, Maria. What happened to you? Did someone hurt you?"

I nodded curtly, glancing down at my arms. The bruises formed a dark rainbow that looked quite disturbing. No wonder these humans were so shocked.

"What happened to the men who did this?"

I hesitated for a moment, before deciding to be honest. Let her fear me a little. "Sharks." I felt my face lift in a grin.

"Sharks?" she repeated.

I nodded. I thought of Sciarra screaming as the sharks tore him to pieces and only wished the brutish Barrett could have shared his fate. I was far more dangerous than any shark and the fish knew it, too. "Sharks."

To my surprise, she burst out laughing. "I can't say I'm sorry. I think you and I are going to get along fine, Maria. I'm Meryl D'Angelo, but you can call me Aunt Merry. Let's get some arnica on those bruises and I'll see if I can find you some clothes. I have boxes of them from my friends and relatives in England to donate to the poor people in Australia.

They'll be poorer still once they see the outdated fashions I have. Some of these are older than me!" She laughed again, before gesturing at me. "Stand up and take that piece of sailcloth off. Let me look at you so I can work out what might fit you."

Perhaps for the first time in my life, I obeyed. I rose to my feet and let go of the salt-stiffened sail, which slipped to the floor. Her horrified gasp made me look down. The sordid rainbow across my broken ribs made my eyes water.

"With breasts like that, it's probably a good thing I have some fashions from a few years ago," she managed to say. "If I put you in one of the flapper dresses my nieces were wearing, men wouldn't be able to stare at anything but your chest. So, are you ready to have some fun?" She dropped to her knees by one of the boxes on the floor and flipped open a clasp. Lifting the lid, she pulled out ruffled, frilly garments like those she was wearing.

I shrugged off the shredded shirt that was

all I had left from the *Trevessa* and braced myself. Women's clothing and a willing teacher. She offered me everything I wanted…except for the one thing I wanted most. William. With a heavy heart, I took the garments she offered and clothed myself in another new life.

The story continues in
*Ocean's Widow*

# ABOUT THE AUTHOR

Demelza Carlton has always loved the ocean, but on her first snorkelling trip she found she was afraid of fish.

She has since swum with sea lions, sharks and sea cucumbers and stood on spray drenched cliffs over a seething sea as a seven-metre cyclonic swell surged in, shattering a shipwreck below.

Demelza now lives in Perth, Western Australia, the shark attack capital of the world.

The *Ocean's Gift* series was her first foray into fiction, followed by her suspense thriller *Nightmares* trilogy. She swears the *Mel Goes to Hell* series ambushed her on a crowded train and wouldn't leave her alone.

Want to know more? You can follow Demelza on Facebook, Twitter, YouTube or her website, Demelza Carlton's Place at:

www.demelzacarlton.com

# Books by Demelza Carlton

## Siren of Secrets series

Ocean's Secret (#1)

Ocean's Gift (#2)

Ocean's Infiltrator (#3)

## Siren of War series

Ocean's Justice (#1)

Ocean's Widow (#2)

Ocean's Bride (#3)

Ocean's Rise (#4)

Ocean's War (#5)

How To Catch Crabs

## Nightmares Trilogy

Nightmares of Caitlin Lockyer (#1)

Necessary Evil of Nathan Miller (#2)

Afterlife of Alana Miller (#3)

## Mel Goes to Hell series

The Devil's Work (#1)

See You in Hell (#2)

Mel Goes to Hell (#3)

To Hell and Back (#4)

The Holiday From Hell (#5)

All Hell Breaks Loose (#6)

The Devil Goes to Heaven (#7)

## Romance Island Resort series

Maid for the Rock Star (#1)
The Rock Star's Email Order Bride (#2)
The Rock Star's Virginity (#3)
The Rock Star and the Billionaire (#4)
The Rock Star Wants A Wife (#5)
The Rock Star's Wedding (#6)
Maid for the South Pole (#7)
Jailbird Bride (#8)

## Romance a Medieval Fairytale series

Enchant: Beauty and the Beast Retold
Dance: Cinderella Retold
Fly: Goose Girl Retold
Revel: Twelve Dancing Princesses Retold
Silence: Little Mermaid Retold
Awaken: Sleeping Beauty Retold
Embellish: Brave Little Tailor Retold
Appease: Princess and the Pea Retold
Blow: Three Little Pigs Retold
Return: Hansel and Gretel Retold
Wish: Aladdin Retold
Melt: Snow Queen Retold
Spin: Rumpelstiltskin Retold
Kiss: Frog Prince Retold
Reflect: Snow White Retold
Roar: Goldilocks Retold
Cobble: Elves and the Shoemaker Retold